"Does Mr. Duff think Evie's a dyke?"

"I hate that word, Parr. . . . Someone like Evie gets the blame when there's any suspicion of such a thing."

"Do *you* think she's one?"

"That's crossed my mind, Parr. You've heard me nagging at her to be more of a lady."

"What if she is one?"

"It's going to be very hard for her, if she is."

"It'll be hard for both of them, won't it?"

"It'll be harder for Evie. Evie can't pass herself off as something else. It isn't in her nature."

"No," I said. "It isn't."

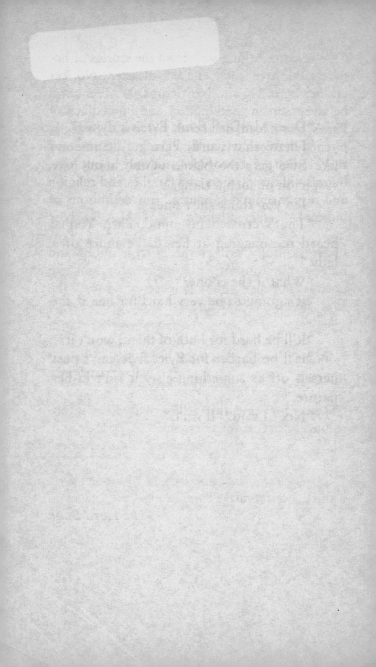

BOOKS BY M. E. KERR

Dinky Hocker Shoots Smack!
Best of the Best Books (YA) 1970–83 (ALA)
Best Children's Books of 1972, *School Library Journal*
ALA Notable Children's Books of 1972

If I Love You, Am I Trapped Forever?
Honor Book, *Book World* Children's Spring Festival, 1973
Outstanding Children's Books of 1973, *The New York Times*

The Son of Someone Famous
(AN URSULA NORDSTROM BOOK)
Best Children's Books of 1974, *School Library Journal*
"Best of the Best" Children's Books 1966–1978,
School Library Journal

Is That You, Miss Blue?
(AN URSULA NORDSTROM BOOK)
Outstanding Children's Books of 1975, *The New York Times*
ALA Notable Children's Books of 1975
Best Books for Young Adults, 1975 (ALA)

Love Is a Missing Person
(AN URSULA NORDSTROM BOOK)

I'll Love You When You're More Like Me
(AN URSULA NORDSTROM BOOK)
Best Children's Books of 1977, *School Library Journal*

Gentlehands
(AN URSULA NORDSTROM BOOK)
Best Books for Young Adults, 1978 (ALA)
ALA Notable Children's Books of 1978
Best Children's Books of 1978, *School Library Journal*
Winner, 1978 Christopher Award
Best Children's Books of 1978, *The New York Times*

M.E. KERR

Deliver Us From Evie

HarperTrophy®
A Division of HarperCollinsPublishers

Harper Trophy® is a registered trademark
of HarperCollins Publishers Inc.

Deliver Us From Evie
Copyright © 1994 by M.E. Kerr
All rights reserved. No part of this book may be used or reproduced in
any manner whatsoever without written permission except in
the case of brief quotations embodied in critical articles and reviews.
Printed in the United States of America. For information address
HarperCollins Children's Books, a division of HarperCollins Publishers,
10 East 53rd Street, New York, NY 10022.

Library of Congress Cataloging-in-Publication Data
Kerr, M. E.
    Deliver us from Evie / M.E. Kerr.
        p.   cm.
    Summary: Sixteen-year-old Parr Burrman and his family face some
difficult times when word spreads through their rural Missouri town
that his older sister is a lesbian, and she leaves the family farm to live
with the daughter of the town's banker.
    ISBN 0-06-024475-5. — ISBN 0-06-024476-3 (lib. bdg.)
    ISBN 0-06-447128-4 (pbk.)
    [1. Lesbians—Fiction.   2. Family life—Missouri—Fiction.
3. Farm life—Missouri—Fiction.   4. Missouri—Fiction.]   I. Title
PZ7.K46825De   1994   94-1296
[Fic]—dc20   CIP
                                                                     AC

Typography by Stefanie Rosenfeld
◆
First Harper Trophy edition, 1995.

For Robert O. Warren,
skillful editor,
fast walker,
smooth talker . . .
with thanks for years of help.

Deliver Us From Evie

1

Pig Week begins the first Monday after Labor Day at County High.

The freshmen and the transfers from Duffton School are "the pigs."

The seniors are out to get you. They call "SOU-weeeee! Pig, pig, pig!" at you, and they put you in a trash can, tie the lid with rope, and kick you around in it. You learn how to curl into a ball and cover your head with your arms. That happened to me first thing in the morning. I was a transfer junior from Duffton.

Then, in the afternoon, a few got me by my locker. They read my name on the door, PARR BURRMAN, and one of them said, "Hey, we know your brother. What's his name again?"

"Doug Burrman," I said.

They said, "Not *that* brother! Your other brother."

"I only have one brother," I said.

They said, "What about Evie?"

Then they began to laugh. They began to say things like "You remember *him*, don't you? Doesn't he live with you? Sure he does! The Burrman brothers: Doug, Parr, and Evie!"

I didn't mention it when I got home.

"How'd things go, Parr?" my mother said.

"Okay. I'm glad Doug warned me about how to curl up in that trash can."

"Did they make you roll in the mud?"

"They didn't have any mud today—but they said we'd better not wear our good clothes tomorrow."

"Ah, well, I guess they'll have the pigpen ready tomorrow." My mother had a tuna fish sandwich ready for me before I changed and went out to do my chores. She said, "They never gave a warning to Doug or Evie. You should have seen their clothes!"

Mother was the reason I was named Parr.

She'd been Cynthia Parr when she met Dad at the University of Missouri. He'd been in the Agricultural College there.

Now my brother Doug was following in his footsteps. Of the three of us—me, almost sixteen; Evie, eighteen; and Doug, twenty—I was the only one who didn't want to be a farmer.

I could hear the combine working its way through the field out behind the house. I knew Evie was driving the thing. It'd grab the entire plant of corn, strip off its ears, take the kernels, pump them into a storage tank, and dump the rest of the plant back into the field behind it.

Sometimes I'd look at my mother and wonder how she'd ever brought someone like Evie into the world.

The only thing they had in common was a love of reading. Evie wrote some, too, like Mom used to when she was her age. But they weren't alike in any other way. They didn't even look alike. Evie had Dad's height—she was almost six foot—and she had Dad's brown hair instead of being blond like Mom.

You'd say Evie was handsome. You'd say Mom was pretty.

Then there was the difference in the way both of them dressed.

My mother wasn't like most farm women, who wear jeans and sweatshirts. She had a few pairs of slacks, but mostly she wore skirts or dresses, and the only time I ever saw her in men's clothes was sometimes when we were harvesting. She'd bring some sandwiches out to us and she might have on an old shirt of Doug's or my father's gloves, maybe my boots, but she was as uncomfortable in men's things as Evie seemed to be in female stuff.

I knew Mom would hate it if I told her the kids had called Evie my brother.

She was trying hard to change Evie that fall, trying everything, but it was like trying to change the direction of the wind.

2

Halloween night the Duffs always invited everyone from nearby farms to come to theirs.

Our town got its name from the Duffs. Their family had founded it way back.

They had a thousand acres. We had a hundred and fifty.

Mr. Duff was a banker, too, and he held the mortgage on most of the farms that weren't paid off yet, including ours.

Evie didn't want to go to the party. Way past dark she was still out in the middle of a back field fooling around with a balky diesel engine, welding something that had broken.

My father said let her stay there, what the heck, but my mother insisted Evie come in and change her clothes and go with us.

I could hear them arguing upstairs while my father

sat in front of the TV, watching news of hog and corn futures broadcast on *The Farm Report*.

"It'd fit you, Evie!" my mother was telling her.

"It might fit me but it doesn't suit me!"

"Try it, that's all."

"Wear a skirt to the Duffs'? I don't care about the Duffs! That's your problem, not mine!"

"What's my problem, Evie?"

"Wishing you were high class is your problem!"

"I am high class."

"You *were* high class, maybe, back when you were a Parr. Now you're just a farmer's wife, Mother—get used to it!"

My father could hear them, too.

He said to me, "Tell those two we're not going anyplace if they don't get down here right now."

I called up, "So long! We're leaving."

My mother came downstairs in a long black skirt with black boots and a white silk blouse. Her blond hair spilled down to her shoulders, and she had on pearls my father'd bought her back when they first got married.

I was in jeans, boots, and a white shirt.

My dad was in jeans, boots, and a flannel shirt.

When Evie appeared she was in jeans, boots, and a heavy sweatshirt that said GET HIGH ON MILK! OUR COWS ARE ON GRASS!

She wore her hair very short, with a streak of light blond she'd made with peroxide. That was as close as she'd ever come to makeup. She'd written one of her nonrhyming poems about it. (Mom called them "statements.") It began *There's only a ribbon of color I put in my black-and-white life./Combed back you can hardly see it, just like my black-and-white life.*

She cocked her hand like a gun and shot at me.

"Let's go!" she said.

You could see the blue of her eyes all the way across a room. I thought she looked a little like Elvis Presley.

My father guffawed when he saw the sweatshirt. "Where'd you get that thing?"

Evie always talked out of the side of her mouth. "I got it out at the mall. Like it?"

"Evie," my mother said, "it's not appropriate to wear to the Duffs'."

"Why isn't it appropriate?" my father said. He wasn't crazy about the Duffs, for one thing; for another, he always took up for my sister.

My mother liked to say that's how Evie got to be the way she was. She only listened to my father. Listened to him, walked like him, talked like him, told jokes like him.

While Evie drove us over to the Duffs', Dad started griping about The Duffton National Bank, and how hard they were on the farmers who got behind in their mortgages.

"These are hard times for everybody," my mother said.

Evie said, "Only difference between a pigeon and a farmer today is a pigeon can still make a deposit on a John Deere tractor."

My father let out a hoot and gave her back a slap.

"Where'd you hear that one?" he asked, laughing.

In the backseat, beside me, my mother just sighed.

3

We never saw much of Patsy Duff because she went to private school and summer camp, but she was home for a long weekend.

I watched her that night and thought of that case, a while back, about the babies being switched in the hospital, each one going home to the wrong family.

Patsy looked enough like my mother to be her daughter. Her blond hair fell down her back and she had that same flirty quality my mother had with people, smiling easily into their eyes, listening nicely, and saying the right things back. She had class, like my mother, and seemed older than seventeen.

"Your husband's so handsome, Mrs. Burrman," she told my mother, passing her a mug of cider.

"Oh, Douglas would like to hear that," said my mother.

"I heard you met him in college."

Then my mother went into her story about how she never expected to date an ag student, how she always imagined she'd go for a law student or a journalism student, but Douglas just swept her off her feet, she guessed it was those dimples of his, that smile, instant chemistry, she said, and here I am on a farm in Missouri when I always thought I'd be working for a New York City newspaper.

"Were you in journalism school?" Patsy asked, and my mother nodded.

I hung around in the background, smiling. I wasn't unlike my dad in looks. I was tall and skinny as he was, no dimples but a good smile when I smiled. I didn't often smile *at* people, as he did. That was more Evie's style. She'd walk right up and glad-hand them and grin at them.

I stood there hoping Patsy Duff would look my way.

My mother read my mind and said to Patsy, "Have you met my son Parr?"

"Hello, Parr," Patsy said. She had on a white wool skirt and a red sweater. "Excuse me, please, Mother may need some help 'long about now."

I watched her walk away. At one end of the large room Evie was down on her knees with her head in a pail of water, ducking for apples, while all the little kids there laughed and clapped.

At the other end of the room the men were gathered around Mr. Duff. He was short and fat, his red face cut with a wide white smile. He had on a blue blazer with gold buttons, and a white turtleneck sweater. He never looked like anyone else in Duffton. Neither did his farm. There was a swimming pool behind the house, and he always had a new-that-year sports car parked in the garage. And not that he ever personally drove a tractor, but if he felt like it there were several of the latest enclosed air-conditioned International Harvesters out near his barn. His help had it real good at Duffarm, which is what the gold sign out front said.

It wasn't that Mr. Duff didn't do good things for the town; he did. There was the Duffton Municipal Swimming Pool he'd paid for; there was the Duffton Community Center. And there was the Veterans' Memorial Statue, center of town—a stone guy in a helmet, charging with a fixed bayonet.

Kids hung things on the bayonet nights they roamed homeward from the movie or the bowling alley. A rubber chicken, a bra, a rubber tire—you never knew what you'd see hanging off it first thing in the morning.

I saw some guys I'd gone to Duffton School with, ones who didn't finish over at County High, dropouts, farming now. Most of them had their own pickups, and they seemed older than me suddenly, talking farm stuff while they shot pool in Mr. Duff's rec room. I hung out with them. Some of them planted and harvested for us, since Doug was in college. One of them was Cord Whittle, who had a crush on Evie. He kept talking about how she could do anything a man could do, then he nudged me and said, "Well, *almost!*"

We didn't stay late.

Dad had an appointment early the next morning with someone from the Rayborn Company. They serviced farms with things like stacked cages for chickens that never got outside, layers that lived several birds to a cage and never even saw a rooster. Modern farming! It made Mom and me sick to think about it. But Dad wasn't going into the chicken business. If anything, we'd cut way back on all livestock but hogs. We had new ones from Europe that were supposed to produce a lean, low-cholesterol pork, since the whole country seemed to be on a health kick.

Dad just wanted a part-time sales job to help us

along. When Mom said she'd just as soon get a job, he asked her what she thought she already had—keeping our books, running our farm.

He wanted Evie to go to the university, too, when he could spare her. Ag school like Doug, so she'd be up on all the new techniques, like learning about the soybean plants they grew in China, ones that could take a good ground soaking better than ours . . . That was behind his job hunt, too—Evie's education.

On the way home Mom suddenly noticed Evie had on a different sweatshirt. It was white with a gold seal that said APPLEPERSON ACADEMY.

"Where's *your* shirt, Evie?"

"I got it wet. Patsy lent me this, and then we decided to trade shirts. This is her school shirt."

"I thought she went to Appleman Academy."

"She does. But the students call it Apple*person* Academy, for fun. You know, Mom, you're supposed to say spokesperson for spokesman, and chairperson for chairman. You can't be sexist."

Dad chuckled and said, "Does that make us the Burrpeople?"

"I guess we *should* change our name," Evie said. "Patsy said her little nieces and nephews can't play cowboys and Indians, anymore, either. They have to play cowpeople and Native Americans."

"She's such a lovely girl," said Mom. "I tried to get something going between you two tonight, but I couldn't seem to do it, could I?"

Evie's face got red. "Why would you try to do that?" she snapped, and she almost drove off the road. "What did you say to her?"

There was a pause before my mother said, "I didn't mean between *you* and Patsy, Evie. I meant between Parr and Patsy."

No one said anything for a while.

Then my dad said, "Parr's got a case on Toni Atlee, anyway. He doesn't want some girl goes miles away to boarding school."

I said, "I wouldn't mind, but I'd never get to first base with her kind."

Evie didn't say anything the rest of the way home.

At Thanksgiving Doug came home from college for the weekend, bringing this sorority girl with him.

She was a Tri Delt named Bella Hanna, and I doubt she'd ever been on a farm before.

I think everyone in our family except Doug was thinking the same thing: Don't let her be the one.

She was this redheaded princess who didn't offer to do anything to help Mom get the dinner on, and anytime Doug said he wanted to show her something out back, she'd say, "Do we have to?"

Mostly she sat in the living room reading magazines she'd brought with her: the thick kind filled with fashion ads and the sweet-smelling inserts Mom liked to tear out and put in her underwear drawer. When Evie told Bella Hanna Mom liked to use them for that, she just shrugged and said she never heard of someone doing that. She didn't offer any of them to Mom.

Later I heard her ask Doug if Evie was "all right" and Doug said, "What do you mean?"

"Well, she seems a little odd, the way she dresses and stuff."

"She's a farmer!" Doug said, and he laughed and got red.

"If that's what happens when you're a farmer, spare me," she said.

"Evie's okay," Doug said.

I could remember when Doug would punch out guys who made any cracks about Evie around him. Next to Dad, Doug was Evie's main defender: She was his kid sister he didn't take any lip about. But Bella Hanna was different. She had Doug wrapped around her little finger. He was actually worried about things like were we going to use linen napkins for dinner, and not paper ones. And who was Mom going to sit on the other side of Bella—not Cord Whittle, he hoped!

Mom said, "Cord's not even invited. Evie doesn't want him here."

"Good!" Doug said, relieved.

"What have you got against Cord, Doug?"

"He's a real hick, Mom! If Bella got stuck with that dropout, she'd think that's what farmers are like."

"He's a good farmer, Doug!"

"Yeah, well Melvin's got more sense!"

Melvin was our mule. Evie claimed Melvin was the type of animal who'd work patiently for ten years for the chance to kick you once hard.

I'd never seen my brother in the state he was in. It was as threatening to me as a dark funnel in a pink sky, because I was counting on Doug's decision to farm. As good as Evie was, there was no way she could run our place all by herself . . . and our father was already nearing fifty. If Doug changed his mind—if someone like Bella Hanna changed it for him—there was going to be pressure on me.

We had a dozen relatives come for Thanksgiving

dinner. I was appointed to say grace and I included a line about keeping our farm safe from harm, hoping it'd go from my lips to God's ears, figuring God would know what I was really talking about.

Mom seated one of the little kids next to Bella Hanna and she blossomed, talking baby talk to him, cutting his meat for him, and announcing she wanted a big family. She said there were five in her family, and that she was from Vermont, and she'd come all the way to Missouri to study journalism.

"Oh, I wanted to be a newspaperwoman too," said my mother.

"What happened?" Bella asked her.

"Mr. Burrman," my mother answered.

"So you sold out for love," said Bella.

"I wouldn't put it that way, myself," my mother said.

Bella Hanna said, "Women always used to give up their dreams for men. It's time men gave up theirs for women."

I could see Doug's Adam's apple bob as he swallowed hard, and he pushed a lock of blond hair out of his face.

"Besides," Bella Hanna continued, "you can't make any money farming anymore. That's what I heard."

Evie spoke up then, said, "You can still make a small fortune in farming. Trouble is you have to start with a large one."

My father burst out laughing at that. Then everyone did.

After dinner we were all stuffed, and my father said we should walk out back and see the sky. It was filled with lakes of fire, and everybody was looking up and exclaiming. Pete and Gracie, our yellow Labs, were dancing off toward the fields that were lying fallow now.

Off in the distance a car was coming down our road, a fancy one: You could see the sinking sun making it glisten, and it had the roar of a good motor that ran better fast than slow.

We all began watching its approach . . . all but Evie.

Evie was like a horse that way. A horse never reacts to anything new coming. A cow will throw up its head and stare, and maybe moo and shuffle its feet, but all you see a horse do is prick its ears forward.

I wondered why Evie didn't even look in the direction of the car. I'd never seen a car that color: black cherry it was—a sleek, sexy Porsche.

Mom said, "*Who* is this?"

The only strange cars that ever came our way belonged to Jehovah's Witnesses, chimney sweeps, and land assessors.

When it got closer, I recognized the long blond hair.

She had on dark glasses, and she gave everyone a wave.

"Patsy Duff!" my mother said. "What's she doing here?"

Then Evie turned around and said, "She's here to interview me."

"Who's Patsy Duff?" Bella Hanna said, and you could see she was real impressed . . . with the car, and with the girl getting out of it.

Doug told Bella she was just a friend, as though Patsy Duff came over to our place any old time.

Mom looked at Evie and asked her, "What are you talking about?"

"I forgot to tell you. She called last night to see if she could interview me for her school paper. She wants to do an article about a farmwoman."

"You mean a farm *person*," my father said.

He was straightening his tie as Patsy slammed the car door and started toward us. She had that effect on you: She looked so good you started worrying about how *you* looked.

I wished I hadn't been stubborn and refused to

wear a tie, or my best jacket. I was in a seedy old brown suit because I hadn't wanted to go out of my way for Doug's Tri Delt.

Neither had Evie bothered to dress up. But her white shirt, open at the collar, was clean, and she had on a good belt with a big silver buckle. Jeans and the boots she called her shitkickers.

"Hi, everybody!" Patsy called out. She was wearing a leather skirt and a suede jacket, carrying a notebook, and grinning. "Ready, Evie?"

"Sure thing," Evie called back.

By December we still didn't know any details of Patsy Duff's interview with Evie. She taped it in Evie's room, and we didn't even see Patsy leave because our relatives were still there, and so was Bella Hanna.

We heard the Porsche start up, heard two little honks of good-bye; then Evie took a flashlight out into the fields to bring in the hand-powered posthole digger she'd been using to fix a fence.

We were surprised when we read the interview in

he Appleman Arrow, the school paper Patsy sent to
vie at the beginning of December.

Patsy D. What are you dreams for the future?

Evie B. *I think of having plans, not dreams, but
if I was the sort who had dreams, I'd
wish we could buy out the Atlee land
next to us. They're C.S.& F. farmers,
with the emphasis on the F. lately. He's
out of here at the first frost.*

Patsy D. What's a C.S.& F. farmer?

Evie B. *That stands for corn, soybeans, and
Florida. They go to Florida every winter,
and now the son over there is studying
medicine. I think their place will be up
for grabs sometime in the future.*

Patsy D. So you never think of leaving Duffton,
or this farm?

Evie B. *Well, I am thinking seriously of entering
ag school over at Columbia. I have a lot
to learn.*

Patsy D. You sound real smart to me.

Evie B. *(Laughing hard) Yeah, but you're easy to
impress, aren't you, because what do
you know about all this? I bet you never
even milked a cow.*

19

My mother said to Evie, "How about letting your father and me in on your plans?"

"You're in on them now," said Evie.

"When are you making this big move, Evie?"

"I figure next fall. Dad and I've been talking about it."

Mom sighed. "So that's really why he had that interview with the Rayborn Company last month. . . . Well, if you do it, we'll have to hire extra help."

"*I* can do more than I'm doing now, too," I said, figuring I'd do anything in the short run that'd keep me off the farm in the long run.

But we *would* need to hire help. That was the expensive part of Evie going to college, not college itself. The university didn't cost Missouri residents that much, but Evie did the work of two men.

Then everything changed.

One night Will Atlee came over and told my father he wanted to talk. He said he thought my mother and Evie might like to hear what he had to say, too.

I took Toni Atlee for a sunset walk around our place.

I told her that she was probably the only one in the world who could maybe change my mind about farming.

"If I had someone like you, I could almost see

doing it," I lied. No way would I ever farm, not even for Toni.

She was this five-foot-three brunette with a body that ripped right through you, and a smart mouth. We were sitting in my father's pickup by that time, the motor on for warmth, listening to KKRG, watching a ball of red sneak down through these wispy smoke-blue clouds. She had on something that smelled like lilies.

"What a lot of bull crap, Parr!" she said. "You're no farmer! You just want my bod. And I don't even like farming—don't you know *anything*?"

"Me want your bod? *Me?* I'm trying to plan my future and you're turning it into some kind of sexual fantasy!"

"That arm of yours is creeping around my neck, Parr. How does *that* figure in your future plans?"

My hand landed on her shoulder.

She pushed it away and sat forward. "What a great sunset, Parr!"

"What if I said I was going to study to be a lawyer, probably settle in Kansas City, probably make several hundred thou a year?"

"How about settling in Miami? I'm used to warm winters."

We were laughing. I was reaching out to touch her and she was pushing my hand away.

"Okay, Miami," I said.

She grabbed my hand and held it. "*We're* not farmers, Parr. And anyway, *I'm* moving, Parr. That's what Daddy's inside talking about to your daddy."

"You don't mean you're moving for good?"

She turned her head and looked at me. I loved her eyes, and her smile. "Would I do this if I wasn't?" she said, and she leaned into me and kissed me.

She whispered, "I'd never do that if I was going to stay here in Duffton. It'd only start your motor going."

"What do you think my motor's doing now, standing still?"

"Turn it off," she said. She straightened up and pulled down the door handle, and we were over before we even started.

Mr. Atlee had a deal with my father that made it seem like all our dreams were coming true.

We'd get a hundred of his acres for a song (the rest was going full price to the neighbor on his other side) if we'd run everything for him for five years on a fifty-fifty split of profits. There were all sorts of other conditions, things they'd work out with lawyers, but it was better than a good deal. Even I was excited.

So maybe new dreams cost old ones.

Atlee land in exchange for Atlee daughter.

Everyone in the house was celebrating. My father had opened a bottle of Seven Crowns they were pouring into Seven-Up. Even Evie was having a drink. Evie was giving up something for what we were getting. With the Atlee acres to work, there was no way she'd get to college that next fall.

Evie and my mother stayed in the kitchen having a nightcap after my father went to bed. I was right around the corner, watching TV.

"I'd rather be here, anyway," Evie said. "I think I was just saying all that because that's Patty's world: boarding school, college—she'll probably pledge a sorority like Anna Banana."

"I was a sorority girl too, don't forget. And my sorority was one of the big three, unlike Bella Hanna's." My mother was slurring a little. She wasn't used to drinking liquor. She said, "If you'd gone to Missouri, you'd automatically be a Pi Phi, Evie. You'd be a legacy."

"Yeah, well, they'd be tickled to see me clumping up their front sidewalk, wouldn't they?" said Evie.

"Evie, honey, you could be every bit as pretty as any one of those Pi Phis . . . if you'd just let me help you with your clothes, if you'd just change your hair, *style* it—you could still wear it short. You could—"

Evie cut her off. "I'm the way I am."

"Honey, you look so tough when you smoke that way. If you *have* to smoke, hold the cigarette between your fingers."

There was probably a Camel cigarette dangling from her lips. Evie usually smoked no hands. No one else in our family smoked.

"Some people like me the way I am," Evie said.

"But you don't like *him*," said Mom.

"I'm not talking about Cord Whittle!"

After Mom went up to bed, I asked Evie why she called Patsy Duff "Patty."

"I like Patty better," she said. Then she said she'd written something new, and did I want to hear it?

It was called "Asian Journey."

So what if we've never traveled together,
Your blond hair blown by some runway wind,
My hand under your arm as another excuse to touch
    you in public,
To touch you anywhere.
Your eyes reflecting my smile, my dead serious
    expression, our amazement at everything in China.
So what if we've never been anywhere together,

Just seen each other once or twice,
Just talked together on the telephone.

"What's it mean?" I said. "You've never been to China."

"That's the point. It's all in the imagination."

"Is it supposed to be about Patsy Duff?"

"It's all in the imagination," said Evie. "It's not about anyone."

I figured she was bombed or she wouldn't have read it to me.

But maybe something was going on with her that was just bursting to come out.

6

Near Christmas we always got a bunch of calendars sent to us. They came from the bank, the mortician, real estate firms, feed companies—I found about five of them in the mailbox one December afternoon after I got off the school bus.

I flipped through the mail going up our driveway; the calendars were most of it, a few bills, and a postcard I thought might be from Doug.

It said:

Here for the weekend with Margaret Leighton,
whose father owns this place.
 Wish you were her.
      P.
P.S. See you soon!

It took me a few seconds to realize it wasn't from my brother. It was addressed to Evie. On the front was a picture of a Mississippi steamboat that was really a restaurant called Leighton's, in St. Louis.

It also took me a while to register the fact it didn't say *Wish you were here* but *Wish you were her.*

I thought about it while I let myself into the house and shouted out to Mom I was home. She was in the kitchen, where she always was when I got home from school. I stuck the postcard in my English lit book and left it on the stairs with my gym bag.

"Looks like snow outside," Mom said.

"About time, isn't it?" I dropped the bills and the calendars on the kitchen table, and she sat down and riffled through everything.

I poured myself some milk and took some cookies from the jar.

"We're having company for dinner," she said.

"How come?"

"I asked Cord Whittle over."

"How *come*?"

"Well, he might be interested in helping out with the Atlee place."

"That's way next spring."

"And it's Friday. I have a lamb roast in. Anyone you'd like to invite over?"

"She's in Miami," I said. "Since when do we have dinner parties on Friday night?"

"I'm celebrating," Mom said. "I got Evie to go to Garden Hairstyles for a cut."

"How did you do that?"

"I won a bet!" Mom laughed. "Remember she bet me that sinkhole out in the far pasture was safe? She bet me whatever I wanted her to do for me that I couldn't push a hoe down it, and I bet her a week's washing chores I could. Then we forgot about it. . . . Melvin's back foot went through it this morning."

"What's Cord Whittle got to do with it?"

"Nothing."

"Does Evie know he's invited?"

My mother shrugged. "Evie doesn't have to know every little thing I plan."

"Stop trying to fix them up, Mom," I said.

"Cord's willing."

"You know darn well Evie's not."

"Last year this time I knew darn well the Atlees farmed next door to us, and now . . ." Mom raised her eyebrow and gave me a look.

I went up to change before I headed down to the barn to feed the hogs.

I stopped off in Evie's room to leave the postcard on her desk.

Usually we left all the mail on the kitchen table, but I didn't feel like doing that. I wasn't sure if I was sparing Mom or Evie.

Both, probably.

7

"**D**on't comb it back, Evie!" my mother said. "It's *supposed* to fall foward."

"It tickles my forehead."

"Your forehead will get used to it."

"I like it, Evie," Dad said. "No fooling."

I liked her new hairstyle too, but it was Dad's saying he liked it that made Evie stick her comb in the back pocket of her jeans and give up trying to slick the cut back the way she always wore it.

"Before Cord gets here," said Mom, "run upstairs and put on my white turtleneck sweater. I ironed it for you and hung it in the bathroom."

"How long am I supposed to pay off this bet?" Evie asked. "I got the haircut, now you're dragging Cord Whittle over here, and next you're telling me what to wear."

"Nobody has to drag Cord over here," said my mother, who was putting candlesticks on the table, on top of the white tablecloth. We were using our good china, too.

"He's coming of his own ac*cord*," Dad said, chuckling at his own joke.

Evie was taking it all in stride, which surprised me some until she followed me upstairs just before I went in to take a shower.

"Did you get the mail, Parr?"

"Don't I always?"

"Did anyone see that postcard besides you?"

"How do you know I saw it?"

"Because you don't usually give me room service."

"Nobody else saw it," I said.

She grinned at me. "Lucky thing you're a snoop."

"Yeah," I agreed. "Lucky thing."

She said, "Thanks, Parr. Hand me Mom's sweater before you get it wet."

It was the postcard that had put her in the good mood.

—

By the time Cord arrived, it was starting to snow lightly. He had a dusting of it on his brown hair when he came inside. He smelled of after-shave, and his hazel eyes were dancing around, as though he imagined it was Evie's idea he'd eat dinner with us.

Under his parka he had on a tan corduroy jacket and a white shirt and bolo tie with a silver clasp. Brown trousers and boots.

He was a good-looking guy. He'd put on some weight. All the dropout farmers did after a while. He had a bottle of preserves his mother'd put up that he gave to Mom, and he had a small stack of old *National Geographic*s for Dad. My father loved looking through travel magazines. The only thing he watched on TV besides sports and the farm reports was PBS specials about places like Africa and Australia. Nobody in our family had ever been outside the United States.

Evie came downstairs in her jeans and Mom's sweater, sporting her new haircut, and Cord said, "Your hair's changed."

"Nothing else has, though," Evie said. I suppose that was her way of warning him not to get his hopes up.

Mom lighted the candles, and we all sat down to

eat Elijah, who'd been our last lamb. He'd been in the freezer since summer, when even Evie'd protested his necessary murder. Elijah, we all swore, could smile and was more like a household pet than something you end up eating with mint jelly.

I was always bored out of my gourd with what Cord and Evie talked about. My mother was off somewhere in her head, and I was chewing away on Elijah and telling myself this was more proof I wasn't cut out for farming, because farming was really a lot about killing, even when you kept the livestock to a minimum—you still had to slaughter some poor thing or send it out to someone else to slit its throat.

I'd tune in and out of the conversation.

Cord would be saying he'd spent the whole afternoon adjusting the idle and the transmission on his IH, while Evie'd agree they were all troublesome, she'd only have a Deere.

"Evie can fix anything, though," my father'd pipe up.

"Not this sucker, not even Evie."

"Wanna bet?" from Evie.

Then the three of them began talking about putting in some other kind of crop on the Atlee acreage, and Evie made her usual complaint about how ugly soybeans always looked. She preferred corn.

She'd even heard you could make good money growing flowers.

"I'd like to look into what the Rayborn Company's selling, Douglas," said Cord through a mouthful of mashed potatoes.

"You don't want layers, do you? They live out their lives in stacked cages, three or four to a cage. I sell the equipment, but that's not my kind of farming."

"Your kind's too much at the whim of Mother Nature."

"Any kind is at her whim in the long run."

"Livestock's not. You ought to double the size of your hog operation, maybe do more breeding, too. Isn't Doug studying animal science over at the university?"

Evie said she favored more hogs too, but we'd need more farrowing crates and ventilation equipment, on and on, until finally Mom and I were clearing and the apple pie was warming in the oven.

I was helping Mom with the dishes after and Dad was in reading one of the *National Geographic*s. Evie and Cord were sitting at the kitchen table talking.

Mom whispered to me, "You go up to your room, Parr. Daddy and I are going to go over the accounts in the office."

I knew she was planning to leave the living room empty for Cord and Evie.

When she'd finished stacking the last plate, she said, "Whew! Evie! The smoke from your cigarettes is too heavy in here."

Evie said, "I'm going upstairs, anyway."

"You don't have to go upstairs," Mom said. "Just move into the parlor."

"You smoke like a chimney," Cord said. "You come on into the parlor with me and I'll tell you how I kicked the habit. . . . You know who was in Smokenders with me? Buck Duff! He was a three-pack-a-day man. How many packs do you smoke, Evie?"

"I got Buck Duff beat."

"Evie!" my mother said. "You don't smoke more than three packs a day!"

"Just kidding," Evie said. "Buck Duff ought to send his wife to Drinkenders."

"She tried Alcoholics Anonymous, I heard," said Cord.

"If it's 'anonymous,' how'd you hear it?"

"Word gets around, Evie."

"Is that why we never see much of her? She drinks?" Mom asked.

"Like a fish," Evie said.

"She's a real nice lady, though," said Cord.

"Halloween night she disappeared," said Mom.

"Up to her room," Evie said. "With a vodka bottle."

"He's a hard man to live with, I bet," said Cord.

"For example?" said Evie.

My mother said, "Now why are we gossiping about the Duffs? You two go in the other room."

I could hear Evie persisting, "For example?" as they pushed back their chairs and went into the other room.

I couldn't hear Cord's answer.

Once my mother got Dad to put down the *National Geographic*, her plan to get Evie and Cord off alone was ruined by Dad's never-ending curiosity about the weather.

He went right to the window when he got out of his chair, gave a look, and said, "You better get going, Cord. Snow's coming down hard."

Immediately Evie walked back into the kitchen and took his parka down from the hook.

"Here's your hat what's your hurry?" Cord said in a miffed tone. "I've got the Jeep. I'm not going to get snowbound."

But Evie was holding the coat up for him to put his arms into. She said, "What would be the difference if a skunk died on the road or Mr. Duff did?"

"I don't know. You tell me."

"There'd be skid marks by the skunk," Evie said.

And my dad howled.

Evie could always break him up.

8

"I don't understand why Patsy Duff would invite you to a concert in St. Louis!" my mother said.

"Maybe she wants to thank me for giving her that interview," Evie said. "She got an A plus on it."

The three of us were having breakfast. Dad had already gone into Duffton, where he was seeing Mr. Duff about a loan. He wasn't going to sell Rayborn products now. Since the Atlee deal he was talking more hogs, breeding, all the things Cord and he had discussed a week ago.

You'd never know Evie's hair had been styled. It was slicked back the old way again. She was chain-smoking over her coffee and reassuring Mom she'd still make it to St. Luke's on Christmas Eve. The concert was the twenty-third.

It promised to be a strange Christmas, anyway. Doug was going to Vermont with Bella Hanna, whom we all called Anna Banana now, thanks to Evie.

Christmas was Mom's favorite holiday, and she counted on the five of us doing the same thing every year: mass on Christmas Eve, then home to trim the tree. Up early Christmas morning for gift giving and breakfast cooked by Dad, the only meal he ever made. Doug and I helped him. After, Evie cleared the table and did the dishes.

Mom wasn't supposed to lift a finger on Christmas morning.

Evie lit a new Camel from an old one and said, "We'll drive in to St. Louis on the twenty-third, stay over, and come back the next morning."

"Stay over where?"

"Some friend of Patty's has a place in Webster."

"What are you going to wear, Evie?"

"My khaki trousers, my blue blazer, something like that."

"To a *concert*? Evie, you have to wear a skirt! Patsy Duff will surely wear a dress to a concert!"

"Not this concert. It's not chamber music, Mom—it's Biker Pike."

"I never heard of him," Mom said. "Is he a rock star?"

"It's a she. She does women's stuff."

"Is she like Judy Collins? I used to love her songs."

"Yeah, something like her. Nobody will dress up, believe me."

"Evie," my mother said, "even if nobody dresses up, I doubt there'll be anyone wearing men's trousers. I have a pair of good gabardine slacks I've hardly worn. Try them on, honey. I can let them out or let the cuffs down, if necessary."

Evie said, "Cork it, Mom."

"Don't speak that way to me. I'm trying to help you!"

I piped up then. "Will you two knock it off? Mom, let Evie off the hook for once!"

I was tired of Mom always on Evie's case. I doubted she even got it. I got it, in a way. What I got was this blurred picture of Evie and Patsy with a crush on each other. It was blurred because that sort of thing was never clear to me, and I wasn't even sure what that sort of thing really meant.

Dad had a distant cousin who farmed in Quincy, Illinois. Cousin Joe. Dad called him Cousin Josephine because he'd lived on a farm with another old man for thirty years. They were a couple, Dad said—"a couple of fruits." I remember Dad watching their pickup come down our road on a visit once telling Mom, "Cousin Josephine's here with his wife," then laughing, and ducking Mom's palm as she tried to swipe him.

I never thought much about them, and when the

thing with Evie and Patsy started, I didn't think they were the same way. Evie was just impressed by Patsy Duff, and I knew by then the feeling was mutual. I didn't take it beyond that point. I wasn't sure Mom had even got that far yet.

Mom blew Evie's smoke away from her face and stood up to put the dishes in the dishwasher. She said, "I'm sorry, Evie, if I seem to nag. . . . I guess you know Patsy Duff better than I do."

"And you know *me*," Evie said. "I am what I am."

Mom said, "I thought that was Popeye the Sailor Man."

"Hey," I said, "Mom made a joke!" and I grabbed my books and my gym bag and headed out to catch the school bus.

I thought about Evie on my way to County. This was the first time she'd connected with anyone where the feeling was mutual.

When she wasn't working around our place, she either had her nose in a book or she played backgammon with Mom, Monopoly with me and Mom, or blackjack with Dad.

She had her second-hand Pontiac; but she didn't use it much except to drive over to the library at King's Corners. She let me drive it around the farm, and the roads close by, but I wouldn't be able to get a license until my birthday in May.

I wasn't the loner she was, but I hadn't made any real friends at County yet either.

When you lived on a farm, you couldn't stay around school after the last class, and do sports or hang out.

You were always needed at home.

So good for Evie, I thought.

There was someone in her life now besides Cord Whittle. . . . But I did, now and then, keep trying to remember the poem she'd written called "Asian Journey."

I wasn't sure I'd heard right . . . the part about touching.

I figured I'd take her at her word—it was just imaginary. And for sure she hadn't been to China.

9

St. Louis got hit hard by a snowstorm on the morning of the twenty-fourth, and Evie phoned to say they were stuck there, probably until Christmas morning.

Mom had a long face after Doug called, just before we left for church.

"This isn't much of a Christmas," she said as Dad

drove us past the snowdrifts, headed into St. Luke's. The Duffs were Episcopalians, so that was the only church in town. A lot of Dufftonites drove over to King's Corners to go to the Catholic church or the First Baptist.

"What do you mean this isn't much of a Christmas?" asked Dad. "How do you think that makes Parr and me feel?"

"You're right, Douglas. I'm not going to ruin things."

"Speaking of ruining things," Dad said, "the Church of the Heavenly Spirit burned down last night. Of all times to have it happen! Some of them will be in our church tonight."

"I *heard*," said Mom. "So we're going to church with the holy rollers."

"Honey, those holy rollers are our neighbors."

"Some of them," she said. "But most of them live over in Floodtown."

Floodtown wasn't much of a town. It'd popped up out of nowhere after the big flood of '73. The river'd washed out this area of bottomland, and all the people living there—many of them tenant farmers or farmworkers living in trailers—moved up and settled in Floodtown. They had a general store and not much else except this shack with a cross on top they'd fixed up as a church.

We went past the Veterans' Memorial Statue, where a Christmas wreath was attached to the end of the bayonet, and when we parked out in front of St. Luke's, we saw that the Duffs were already inside. Mr. Duff's Porsche was there, with "Duffarm" in gold on the door.

Evie'd taken Patsy to St. Louis in her Pontiac.

Before Evie'd left, I'd asked her how come Patsy didn't let her drive the Porsche, and Evie'd answered that it belonged to Mr. Duff, and anyway she doubted he even knew Patsy had invited her to the concert. She'd said Patsy didn't tell her dad her business because he was too controlling. Then I remember she'd added, "But he'll never control Patty, because she's got a will like the river."

I suppose Evie'd made one of her "statements" about it—it was like her to put it that way. I remember a sign Mrs. Cloward tacked up in science that I used to stare at day in and day out, so I'd memorized it without even intending to:

NEVER CAN CUSTOM CONQUER NATURE,
FOR SHE IS EVER UNCONQUERED.

I liked sayings like that: thoughts about Nature and Fate, as though there was an invisible force behind life, something you couldn't see turning you down this road and that, changing your destiny and you.

I wasn't a religious person. I was more like Doug, who said he wasn't an atheist, he wasn't an agnostic, he was an almost. He almost believed. He didn't know what it was he almost believed in, but he almost did.

Like Mom, I liked the ceremony of Christmas. The church was candlelit, and Mr. Duff had paid for all the decorations, as he did every year: pine-branch wreaths and garlands with red ribbons, poinsettia plants everywhere, red and white ones, and an enormous Christmas tree decorated with red and silver bulbs and tinsel, a huge gold star at the top.

We sang all the traditional carols, and we were about a half hour into the service before I saw her.

She wasn't beautiful, not in the same sense that Patsy Duff was. She didn't have the flashiness of Patsy. She didn't even have makeup on. She had long black hair and a pale face, a red velvet dress with a white collar and white cuffs, and this great, clear voice I could hear over all the others: this high strong voice that seemed to be the only sure thing about her. She knew how to sing, and knew she did.

Everyone was looking around to see whose voice it was, but she paid no attention. She was standing between this man and woman who looked on the stern side, plain as white paste, and I knew they had to be from the Church of the Heavenly Spirit.

I also knew I'd been turned down a new path by whatever that force was that I almost believed in.

They say you can stare at the back of someone and they'll eventually feel your eyes on them and turn around to see you. That works if you stare at the side of someone, too.

She was way across the other aisle when I set my mind and my eyes to concentrating on her, and finally she glanced over her shoulder and saw me.

I'd never been so bold in my life, never known the first thing about approaching some girl I just saw somewhere and didn't know anything about. But some instinct got into me, some new, big feeling was pulling me, and I looked right into her eyes, and I nodded at her, and I smiled. I hoped my smile didn't come off like a grimace. I'd never made myself smile in a way there'd be no mistake about it. I'd never faced up to a female in such a manner.

She didn't smile back. I think she frowned a little. I think she wondered what I was doing.

I couldn't take my eyes off her. I watched her through the sermon and the offering, and I knew she felt me doing it.

Then Reverend Southworth gave me the "in" I probably wouldn't have needed anyway, I was so caught up in this new wind. He said, "When we leave here tonight, let us all greet the members of the Church of the Heavenly Spirit, who have joined us for this worship service. Let us let them know we feel the loss of their beloved church, and let us ask them to continue to worship with us for as long as it takes for them to rebuild. A Merry Christmas to all!"

I wanted to get over to her as soon as possible, but Mr. and Mrs. Duff stepped out of their pew just as we were heading down the aisle.

There were the usual hellos and Merry Christmases: Mrs. Duff with her sad eyes, small as he was, thin as he was fat, looking like a little bird afraid of being on the ground.

She and my mother were smiling at each other, shaking hands, and I had my eye fixed on the girl. She was moving slowly between her folks, not looking my way.

Then I head my father's voice boom: "I just hope the roads clear up so those kids get back here tomorrow!"

"What kids?" from Mr. Duff.

"Why, Evie and Patsy," said my father.

"What are you talking about, Douglas?" said Mr. Duff.

I didn't wait to hear the rest of the conversation. I pushed my way past people. I held up my arms and squeezed my way down the aisle sideways. I said, "Excuse me. Excuse me. Merry Christmas to you, too."

I crossed to the aisle she was coming down, and I waited for her.

10

"My name is Parr Burrman," I said. "Merry Christmas, and I'm sorry your church burned down."

She said, "I'm Angel Kidder. Thanks."

"I'm Angel's father, and this is her mother."

I shook hands with her parents. The organ was playing "O Holy Night," and other members of our congregation were reaching out to shake hands with the Kidders too.

Mr. Kidder looked like a young Abe Lincoln, complete with a short, coal-black chin beard. He was tall and blue eyed, not a smiler—none of them were, including Angel. The mother was medium height and pale like Angel, with these round, thick glasses, and a sprig of plastic holly pinned to her coat.

I said, "You have a real nice voice, Angel."

She thanked me without looking at my eyes.

"Angel sings in our choir," her father said.

"She often sings solos," said her mother.

I could see Angel nudging them with her elbow to stop saying stuff about her.

"She was going to sing '"Tick!" Said the Clock' before the fire," said Mrs. Kidder.

"Mama!" Angel protested.

"That's one I don't know," I said.

"You don't sing '"Tick!" Said the Clock' over to this church?" her mother said.

"I never heard it," I said.

"C-L-O-C-K—*The world is like a shelf.* . . . You don't even sing that?"

"No, ma'am," I said. "Maybe one Sunday Angel will sing it here."

"Maybe," said her mother.

Mr. Kidder said, "*I tick, tick, tick, quick, quick.*"

"Oh, Daddy." Angel looked mortified.

We were heading out toward the church entrance where the Reverend Southworth was greeting everyone.

"Where do you go to school?" I asked her.

"King's Corners."

"I go to County."

"I go there next year."

I figured she was fifteen or sixteen. She was carrying a navy-blue duffel coat over her arm. Then she started putting it on and I held it for her.

"My brother went to County," she said. "Now he's at the university."

"Missouri?"

She nodded, and I said, "So's mine. . . . Maybe they know each other."

"He couldn't come tonight. One of the Fultons' sows let down her milk, but she hasn't farrowed yet, so Bud stayed in the barn with her."

"Is your farm in Floodtown?"

"My daddy works on the Fulton farm in King's Corners, and when he's home Bud helps out there, too. But we live in Floodtown. We're in the trailer park there. Sunflower Park."

"We live on a little farm outside of town," I said.

She was zipping up her coat, still not looking at my face.

"But I'm not planning to be a farmer," I said.

"What are you going to be?"

That was the big question, wasn't it? I'd been asking myself that question ever since I'd started in at Duffton School, and I still didn't have an answer.

I said, "I'm going to be anything but a farmer."

"I wasn't born when we lost our place in the '73 flood. The river just ran it down, *pffft*"—she snapped her fingers—"like that. Everything we ever owned got carried off. Daddy said the Lord in his mysterious way doesn't step in at every crisis. He said he never wants to own another farm after that."

"My sister says the river's got a will of its own."

"She's right about that. Don't make any plans for the river, because it's got its own plans, and when the time comes, your plans won't do you any good."

"Have you got a Christmas tree up yet?"

For the first time she laughed. "Up yet? It's Christmas Eve."

"We got it up but not trimmed."

"What are you waiting for?"

"For when we get home."

"We put ours up a week ago and decorated it the same day. I like Christmas. I didn't want to sing '"Tick!" Said the Clock' for Christmas Eve. I wanted to sing a carol, but Pastor Bob said only the whole choir could sing carols or it wasn't fair."

"I never even heard '"Tick!" Said the Clock.'"

"You said you didn't and I was surprised. I thought everyone in the world knew that hymn. It's real old. Eighteen ninety-six. I always find out the date when I learn a hymn, so I know how old it is."

"That's a good idea," I said.

Then Reverend Southworth grabbed Angel's hand.

"Welcome to St. Luke's!" he said.

She told him her name, and I said, "She sings solos, Reverend. She's got a real voice on her!"

"Don't tell him that," Angel said.

"So Parr's been finding out all about you, hmmm?" said the reverend. "Maybe you'll sing for us one Sunday, Angel."

"Well, if you ask me I will, but don't ask me just because *he* said that about my voice. I might not be that good to sing in your church."

"She's that good, all right," said Mr. Kidder with his hand out.

I stepped back to let Mrs. Kidder meet the reverend, and the next thing I knew my mother was pulling at my coat sleeve.

"We're leaving, Parr." She looked cross.

"Wait a minute," I said. "There's someone—"

But she cut me off. *"Now!"* she said.

"What's the matter?"

"What isn't! This is some Christmas!"

"Where's Dad?"

"He's already in the car. Don't make him wait, Parr. He's not in a waiting mood."

I called out, "So long, Angel!"

She was so small I couldn't see her. She was in the middle of a group gathered by the Reverend Southworth.

"Honey, *come*," my mother said.

"Oh, all right! I'm coming!"

"Who's this Angel, anyway?" she said as we started down the front steps into a new, light snow blowing up.

"You'll see," I said.

"Anyone we know?"

"Not yet," I said. "Just I know her."

"This is some Christmas," my mother said again.

I said, "I'll say!" and I was grinning and taking deep breaths of the cold December air, thinking thanks for the Christmas present, Lord, if it was You letting that church burn down last night, in Your mysterious way of not stepping in at every crisis.

Dad made his special eggnog for Mom and him, as he did every Christmas Eve, but this year it didn't seem like fun to be up at midnight trimming the tree and listening to Christmas music.

We strung the lights, but we decided to wait until morning to put on the bulbs and the tinsel.

Dad couldn't stop talking about the way Mr. Duff had bawled him out for letting Evie drive Patsy into St. Louis without his permission, "just as though Evie was a boy or something, trying to date his daughter.

That's what it sounded like!"

"Don't be silly," Mom said. "He's just very protective of Patsy."

"What's he think Evie's going to do to her?"

"He doesn't think Evie's going to do anything to her. He's probably worried about Evie driving."

"So am I worried about Evie driving! So what! It was Patsy's idea to go to that concert! I told him so, too! I told him we weren't very happy about Evie being gone on Christmas Eve, and he said then why'd I let her go? I told him Evie's not a child, and he said Patsy *was*!"

Mom sighed and said, "Come on to bed now, Douglas. It's not Evie's fault that Patsy didn't tell him who she was going with!"

"You know what he said? He said, 'What's that girl of yours up to, if she even is a girl.'"

"I heard."

"What was that supposed to mean?"

"Nothing, Douglas."

"I should have asked him what that was supposed to mean."

"You did right not to."

"He caught me off balance or I would have!"

They finally turned in, and I sat up for a while thinking about Angel and looking in the phone book for the name Kidder.

I found a Nelson Kidder in Floodtown, and I copied down the number. Then I looked in my mother's copy of *Favorite Hymns* for "'Tick!' Said the Clock," but it wasn't there.

Christmas morning about eight o'clock it was blowing more than it was snowing when Cord came by with a present for Evie.

Mom gave him a cup of coffee and told him Dad was down in the barn checking on Melvin, whose foot was still bothering him from when he got caught in the sinkhole.

"I bought Evie a Wynonna tape," Cord said.

"She loves Wynonna. So do I. . . . Did you ever hear of Biker Pike, Cord?"

"He sing Western?"

"It's a she. It's women's music, I think."

"I only know Western. I got Evie a new Ruth Rendell mystery story, too. You say she was at a *concert*?"

"A concert given by this Pike woman."

"I can't keep up with music today," said Cord. "I never figured Evie'd like to go to a concert. I never even knew she was friends with Patsy Duff."

"It's a new friendship," said my mother.

"Well they make a strange pair, don't they? Patsy Duff doesn't give anyone here the time of day."

—

Mom and I trimmed the tree after Cord left. We put his gifts for Evie under it, along with our gifts for each other. Dad made his scrambled eggs and bacon for us, but I was the only one who was hungry. I was the only one with anything to say. I said I'd met this girl named Angel last night in church and I might ask her over if Dad was going anywhere later so we could pick her up.

"Today?" Dad said. "We haven't even had our Christmas, Parr!"

"Won't we be having it after we eat?"

"We'll be having it when Evie ever gets here!" said Dad.

"I doubt that your Angel will want to come over here on Christmas Day, Parr," said Mom. "It's a family day."

"Some family day this year!" Dad snapped.

After we ate, Dad sat in his rocker in the parlor, watching the road from the window.

"I think we ought to open our presents," Mom finally said. "By the time Evie gets here, you're going to be too mad to have Christmas, Douglas."

We were in the midst of gift opening when we heard the Pontiac pull into the driveway.

Pete and Gracie began barking, tails wagging, excited.

Then Evie stamped through the door in Doug's old bomber jacket, with a new red scarf wrapped around her neck and a cigarette dangling from her mouth.

"Ho! Ho! Ho!" she called out. "Merry Christmas, everybody!"

12

We gave each other a lot of music at Christmas. Dad and Evie liked Western tapes. They played them when they were riding around on the tractor or in the pickup or when they were working down in the barn.

Mom liked Western stuff, too, but she was curious about all sorts of other music: Streisand was a favorite, and Whitney Houston, and she liked old Beatles tapes and Elvis ones.

There were several tapes strewn around the parlor with the other gifts.

I think Mom decided music would get us all past the arguing that kept erupting that morning like kernels of corn popping out on a hot pan just when you thought there weren't any left under the ones that'd already blown.

She was fixing a tape in the player after Dad had finished going over his meeting in the church aisle with Mr. Duff again, and Evie'd said again she didn't give a ding-dong-damn what Mr. Duff said!

"She's still in high school, Evie!"—Dad.

"She's one year younger than I am, and a hundred years more experienced than I am!"

"What kind of *experience* are you talking about?"

"Life experience! *Okay?* She's been all over the globe and I haven't even been out of Missouri, unless I was taking hogs to a 4-H show! I'm a hick compared to her! What's he think I'm going to do, turn her into a crack addict or something?"

Dad finally laughed. "I don't know what got into Duff, I swear!"

"Am I a Communist or something, a nudist, a serial killer, a member of a cult or something?"

"I don't know, I swear!"

"Mr. Duff's out of his bird if you ask me!" said Evie.

Then the music began. This female voice began belting out:

> "*They don't call me Pike,*
> *They call me a dyke!*
> *They're right I'm a dyke,*
> *A dyke on a bike—Biker Pike!*"

Evie jumped up from the couch and ran over to the player, her face red, her hand reaching out for the STOP button.

"Don't stop it!" said Dad.

"It's my tape," said Evie, stopping it.

"It was here with the others," said Mom.

"I was playing it in the car. I just put it down there," said Evie. "It wasn't meant for you to hear!"

"I want to hear it!" Dad said. "Did it say what I thought it said?"

"It's just a joke," Evie said. She ejected it and put it in her pocket.

"Let's hear the joke," Dad persisted.

"It's mine," said Evie. "I don't feel like playing it. You'd take it the wrong way. You wouldn't understand it."

"I understand what a dyke is!" my father said. "A dyke is a female Cousin Joe!"

I said, "It's Evie's tape. She doesn't have to play it."

"I'm sorry, Evie," Mom said. "I thought it was the one Cord brought over for you."

"Who gave you that tape? Patsy Duff?" my father said.

"I got it at the concert," said Evie. "It's just a joke."

"What kind of concert *was* that concert?" Mom asked.

"I told you. It was a Biker Pike concert."

"Is *she* a dyke?" my father asked.

"You heard her!"

"Then it's not a joke," Dad said.

"It's meant to be funny," said Evie.

"What's funny about being a dyke?" my father asked.

"I guess what's funny," said Evie, "is that she doesn't care what people say about her."

"That's funny?" he said.

"Never mind, Douglas," said my mother. "It's Christmas."

"Do *you* care what people say about you, Evie?" my father said. "What if somebody got the idea *you* were one of them, because you go to a concert like that? How would *that* set with you?"

"A lot of people went to that concert. They weren't all dykes."

"Hang around with ducks, you start to waddle," said my father.

"Maybe *you* do, Dad." Evie lit a cigarette.

"You *don't*? You don't care if someone gets the idea you're a dyke because you go to a concert like that?"

Evie blew out some smoke. She ran her hand through her hair and stood there shaking her head. She said, "I don't give a ding-dong-damn what people say about me! Okay?"

She started walking toward the stairs.

Dad said, "I don't want you hanging around with Patsy Duff anymore, Evie."

Evie stopped in her tracks. She said, "I'm eighteen years old, Dad. If you're going to suddenly start telling me who I can hang around with and who I can't, I'm out of here!"

Dad backed down. "It's for your own good, honey. I think you're right about Patsy Duff. She is more *experienced* than you are."

Evie said, "Maybe I could use some experience! Maybe I need to see a little more of the world!"

I think Dad felt the same shiver go through him I did.

What in the heck would we do around that place without Evie? Now we had the Atlee land and plans for more hogs, and even Doug seemed to be straying thanks to Anna Banana.

Evie was starting up the stairs.

"Oh, honey," Dad said, "don't go away mad now."

Evie didn't answer him.

I wanted to say: Don't go away at all, Evie. Don't leave me stuck here.

Mom had Barbra Streisand on the player then, singing "We've Never Been in Love Before."

I sat there staring at all the things under the tree: a new sweater and pants for me, the new crock pot Mom had wanted, and the scarf and gloves I'd given her, the Dickey-john soil compaction tester Doug had sent Dad, and the cap I'd got him. There were always new clothes for everyone at Christmas.

Mom had bought Evie some turtleneck sweaters, even though she liked wearing shirts more.

I couldn't think of anything to say. My mind was on Evie, and that song about being a dyke.

Then Mom said, "Why don't you call that Angel up? Wish her a Merry Christmas."

"I wished her that last night," I said. "But I still might do it."

She gave me a smile. "You like short girls, Parr. Toni Atlee was a tiny thing, too."

"She's nothing like Toni Atlee," I said. "Did you hear her singing in church?"

"Who?" said my dad.

"Parr's found himself a girlfriend, I think," Mom said.

"Ah *ha*!" Dad said, and the look on his face was relieved and happy again, and he wanted to know all about her.

13

Next day Dad and Evie and I were counting the hogs we were taking to King's Corners that afternoon. We looked for the ones around two hundred and thirty pounds. We never sold any under that weight, and past two fifty the packing company would dock you for overweight.

"I count twenty," said Evie. "What do you count, Dad?"

"Yeah, about twenty, twenty-two."

I said, "Same here."

It was one job I hated. Sometimes the hogs got stressed out and shit all over you, and they all squealed like they knew right where they were going. I could stand that, but I hated snapping the whip to get them so they'd move aboard the truck, and when Dad had to use the cattle prod I couldn't look.

We'd take good care of them while they were with us, watching over them like they were babies, hauling bales of hay out to the gilts in the south pasture, checking the heating system, their water, all that stuff . . . then the heck with what happened to them when the time came to load them up, all atumble in the truck bed.

Evie and Dad were trying to act normal, but Dad could never fake anything, and his face was down to his boots.

"Well, it'll be a good load," Dad said.

Evie had on jeans and the old leather bomber jacket, but Dad and I wore overalls and heavy flannel shirts with long johns under them. We had on seed caps with the fleece flaps covering our ears, but Evie always went bareheaded in any weather, and jammed her hands into her jeans instead of wearing orange fleece work gloves like we had on.

I was remembering how Mom always told her don't stick your hands in your trouser pockets when you walk, honey, it's so masculine.

Christmas night I'd gone to sleep thinking of things like that—how Mom would always try to change her to be more feminine. And then I'd tried to turn it off by going over my phone call with Angel.

It hadn't lasted long. I could hardly hear her with all the noise in the background. She said all her relatives were over at her place, and said to call her back, or else she'd see me in church on Sunday.

We were coming away from the hog pens, our two yellow Labs running ahead of us, when we heard the car coming and they began barking.

There wasn't another car that came our way that sounded like that, not another car I'd ever seen anywhere the color of black cherries.

Evie stopped to light a cigarette and she didn't even look up, but Dad said, "Now what's she doing here?"

I said, "It's not a she."

Even on this cold gray winter day—the temperature ten degrees Fahrenheit, it'd said when we'd listened over the radio to the morning hog prices—Mr. Duff had the window down all the way, resting his arm on the sill, wearing the big cowboy's Stetson he liked better than the caps every other farmer wore.

"Duff?" Dad said.

"Himself," I said.

He got out of the Porsche and waddled our way while Evie called the dogs back.

Dad said, "Good morning, Mr. Duff." He always called him Mister to his face. Everyone did.

"Morning, Douglas. . . . Morning," nodded at Evie and me.

I said good morning but Evie didn't say anything.

"What brings you over here?" said my father.

"I got something to get off my chest, Douglas."

"Come on up to the house then. Cynnie's got some coffee brewed. We only got decaf, though, I warn you, because Cynnie—"

He cut Dad off. "I'd rather not go up to the house. I'd rather just say what I have to say right here."

We all waited.

"Parr," Mr. Duff said, "you go along to the house."

"I'll go with you," Evie said.

"No, you stay here," Mr. Duff said. "This concerns you, too, Evie."

"Take Pete and Gracie with you," said Dad, so I whistled for the dogs to follow me.

14

"Is that Patsy?" Mom said when I got inside. "She got over here real fast. I just hung up from talking to her."

"It's him, not Patsy."

Mom went to the window. "Mr. Duff? I saw the car coming down the road. I wondered how she could have gotten here when I just put the phone down."

"What'd she call about?"

"She wanted to talk to Evie."

"Maybe she wanted to warn her. He doesn't look like he's in a very good mood. Says he's got to get something off his chest."

"I was afraid of something like this," Mom said.

She'd been working in her office.

Dad always said she was the brains and he was the brawn.

Whenever we got the morning hog prices, she'd call around and see what all the locals were offering, see who could outbid who, start angling for the buyer who'd get our load.

Christmas wasn't an ideal time to sell hogs. Prices went down because folks favored poultry at holidays, but Dad wanted to pay some on the Atlee debt before the first of the year.

"What exactly were you afraid of, Mom?" I followed her into the kitchen.

She began pouring herself a cup of coffee. "Evie," she said. "Mr. Duff's on her case. You know that, Parr."

"I don't know what's going on, though. I thought I did at one time, but now I'm not so sure."

"What'd you think at one time?"

We sat down at the kitchen table.

I said, "I figured Evie and Patsy had this crush on each other."

"What made you come to that conclusion?"

"Evie never had girls for friends, not even when she went to County High. She was always a loner." I wasn't going to tell on Evie: mention the postcard or "Asian Journey." I wanted to see what Mom came up with.

"Evie never had a knack for making friends, of any kind."

"Then Patsy Duff comes along and . . ." I shrugged and didn't finish my sentence.

"It's not Evie's fault," said my mother. "It's Patsy Duff who started this thing."

"What kind of thing is it anyway?" I asked.

My mother let out this long sigh and shook her head. "You called it right, I think. . . . I just hope you did, hope there's nothing really going on, for Evie's sake."

"Does Mr. Duff think Evie's a dyke?"

"I hate that word, Parr. . . . Someone like Evie gets the blame when there's any suspicion of such a thing."

"Do *you* think she's one?"

"That's crossed my mind, Parr. You've heard me nagging at her about trying to be more of a lady. Of course it's crossed my mind."

"What if she is one?"

"It's going to be very hard for her if she is."

"It'll be hard for both of them, won't it?"

"It'll be harder for Evie. Evie can't pass herself off as something else. It isn't in her nature."

"No," I said. "It isn't."

I don't know why I felt relieved to have it spoken, but I did. It was always there, but it was always put another way, as though all Evie needed was to dress up a little more, stop smoking no hands, take smaller steps, get her hair styled—then she'd be no different from anyone else.

It was a relief to tell the truth: to admit that my sister's way wasn't going to be fixed by a turtleneck sweater or a skirt. She was deep-down different.

"If Evie is a lesbian," my mother said, and my stomach did a flip at the harsh sound of that word, "she's got a bigger problem than some other girl would have who isn't so stereotypical."

"Like Patsy Duff. She doesn't seem the type."

"Exactly." Mom sipped her coffee for a moment and then she said, "Parr, don't tell your father about this conversation. Douglas is not a sophisticated man. He won't understand this, if this is what it might be." Then she glanced up at me. "Do you understand it?"

"I understand what a homosexual is because of all the AIDS stuff. But they never talk about females."

"It's not different. It's loving the same sex. Your father's always thought it was a big joke. You know how he makes fun of Cousin Joe."

"I thought they were funny, too."

"I know, Parr." Mom got up and rinsed out her coffee cup. She said, "I just hope Evie has the name without the game. It's bad enough to look that way, but it's awful to look it and actually be it. . . . Then you're a stereotype. You're what everybody's always thought one of those women was like."

"I'm what everybody thinks a farm boy's like. I'm driving around on tractors, going to 4-H, planting in the spring, harvesting in the fall—what's the difference?"

"The difference is you're not against the law, Parr. And the church doesn't call you a sinner."

"Maybe something's wrong with the law."

"It's just not a wholesome thing to be."

"You mean if you *look* it."

"It's better not to, *yes*," said Mom emphatically.

We heard the Porsche leave a moment before we saw Dad and Evie come through the door.

Evie went upstairs without a word.

Dad stood there taking off his gloves and his cap.

"I'd punch him out if we didn't need that bank loan," he said. "You know what he told Evie?" He threw his cap and gloves on the table. "He said she was to stay away from his daughter! He said she was never to write her or try to see her, and get *this*: He said she was never to come anywhere near Duffarm!"

My mother was putting her coffee mug inside the dishwater.

"Did you *hear* me, Cynnie?"

"What did Evie say?" My mother's back was still toward us.

"Evie just took it on the chin! What *could* she say? Evie knows we're working on that loan!"

I said, "I better go out and test the prod. It might need batteries."

If Dad heard me, it didn't register. Nothing registered but what had just happened between Evie and him and Mr. Duff.

I started toward the door.

Mom said, "Have some coffee, Douglas."

"I hate decaf! You get some real coffee for this house by dinnertime or I'll eat down to The Paradise!"

"Why don't you do that?" Mom told him in her quiet voice that meant she was boiling mad too. "Take in a movie while you're at it, Douglas. We won't wait up."

I closed the door behind me.

15

I called Angel twice that afternoon, and that night Angel's mother phoned Mom and asked her if I could go there to Sunday dinner. They'd drive me over after church and Mrs. Kidder would drop me off later that afternoon.

"It pays to advertise," my dad said.

"What does that mean?" Mom asked him.

"That's what Parr's been doing. Advertising himself on the telephone. Right, Parr?"

"I didn't know you'd called her up, Parr."

"Because he was using the barn phone," Dad said. "I knew he wasn't calling here. He was dragging the line all the way down to the cows so I wouldn't hear him."

"And they were mooing," I laughed. "And Angel was saying, 'Where are you, Parr? Out in the pasture?'"

I provided a little badly needed comic relief.

No one was saying anything about Mr. Duff's visit. No one was saying anything much at all, unless they were saying it out of my earshot.

Evie stuck to business, complained that we got taken by the hog buyer, bitched because it'd been her turn to hose out the back of the truck, and allowed as how she'd rather get out of the hog business altogether.

"And live on what?" Dad snorted. "They're our gold."

You'd almost think none of it had happened, except for the red cashmere scarf Evie'd brought back with her from St. Louis. I saw it looped around her bedpost when she wasn't wearing it, which she was, most of the time, except when we did the dirty work of getting the hogs to market.

Sunday morning she wore it to church.

Mom got the bright idea to ask Cord for Sunday dinner, and then, trying to act like it was an afterthought, she'd told him, "Why not join us for the service at St. Luke's beforehand?"

I think she wanted the Duffs to see him with us, with Evie, because she pushed him into our pew next to my sister.

The only trouble was the Duffs weren't at church.

Mom kept looking across at their pew, which stayed empty. I couldn't remember a Sunday without one of them being there.

I kept watching Angel, and she glanced back at me a few times, too.

I could hear her voice, high and sweet through all the hymns, and Dad nudged me once and said, "That gal can sing!"

Bud Kidder, Angel's brother, was there, too. He looked like Abraham Lincoln Jr., with thick black-framed eyeglasses, and he almost drowned Angel out with this big baritone voice.

The Kidders waited to introduce themselves to my folks after the service. Then the five of us squeezed into their little Ford and headed off to Floodtown.

After Mr. Kidder said grace, we ate chicken and dumplings on a table that pulled down out of the wall like a Murphy bed. Bud and Mr. Kidder had a long conversation about the book Bud had got him for Christmas, *The Foremost Mobile Home Fix-It Guide*, until Angel said that I probably didn't want to hear anything about venting roofs or the installation of a tie-down and anchoring system.

"I don't care," I said. "We do a lot of fixing up over at our place, too."

"I know your brother," Bud said. "He's not in my dorm, but I remember him from when we were naming girls we'd like to see be Ag Queen. . . . He wanted some sorority girl for queen, not even from Missouri, much less a farm girl."

"Bella Hanna," I said.

"We kept telling him we didn't want anyone from Sorority Row. No one did."

"You can't tell Doug anything," I said. "He went home with her for Christmas."

"That must have broke your mother's heart," said Mrs. Kidder. "I hope you never do that to us, Bud."

"It wouldn't be for some sorority girl if I did," he said.

"They couldn't *all* be bad," said Mr. Kidder.

"They're not bad, Daddy," Bud said, "they're just snobs. The only time they want to date an ag student is when we have the Harvest Ball and crown the queen. They all want invitations to that. Then they drop us like hot potatoes."

"Are you going to the university when you finish at County?" Mrs. Kidder asked me.

"I plan to."

"He's not going to be a farmer, though," Angel said.

"I wished I'd never been one," said Mr. Kidder.

"You love farming," Bud said. "It was *where* we farmed, not *that* we farmed, broke your heart."

"We didn't have a choice," Mr. Kidder said. "That was our land."

Mrs. Kidder said, "What are you going to do if you don't farm, Parr?"

"I haven't decided yet, ma'am."

"Just don't be a banker," Mr. Kidder said.

"I never would be," I told him. "I wouldn't be good at finances."

"You have to be good at finances and you have to be good at telling people who need something you got it, but they can't get it."

"Like Fat Cat Duff," said Bud.

"No name-calling, Bud," said Mr. Kidder. "Parr here might be a friend of Mr. Duff's."

"Not me," I said.

"I'll tell you something funny about that daughter of his," said Mrs. Kidder. "She come into the store and rented herself a P.O. box in the name of Jane Doe. I thought that was funny. Like John Doe? She paid up for six months, too."

"Where's this?" I asked.

"Mother works over at Barker's General Store in King's Corners," said Mr. Kidder, who called his wife "Mother" just as she called him "Father."

"They have a post office in there," said Mrs. Kidder.

"And the best pies anywhere because Mother bakes them."

"Patsy Duff rented a box there?" I asked. I wasn't sure I'd heard right.

Mrs. Kidder was nodding, but before she could speak, Mr. Kidder said, "Mother, I don't think it's supposed to be public information who rents those boxes."

"Doesn't she go off somewhere to private school?" said Bud. "Over near Jeff City?"

"Father's right," Mrs. Kidder said. "It's none of our business. Forget I said anything about it."

"We're having apple pie for dessert," said Angel. "And *I* made the crust. It's made of graham crackers."

—

Finally, Angel and I got off alone together. We took a long walk around Sunflower Park.

"How come I got invited today?" I asked her.

"Daddy wanted to meet this person ringing me up so much."

"I couldn't help it."

"I know. I was glad."

"Why is that?"

"If you tell me why you couldn't help it, I'll tell you why I was glad."

"Because you're like some new color I've never seen," I said. It was a direct quote from an Evie Burrman "statement." Sometimes she'd leave her notebook somewhere downstairs. I'd sneak fast looks. I almost thought she left it there wanting us to see it. It must have been hard for Evie to try and keep it all inside. I couldn't have.

Angel drew in her breath and shook her head, and let her breath out again. I could see it wisping ahead of us in the cold air. "I'm not that good at putting things," she said.

"I'm not either, Angel. I don't know where that came from."

"From the heart," she almost whispered.

"Yeah," I said softly.

It was nice.

It wasn't like any other moment. We both knew something had happened to us because of each other.

I didn't even care that that was all there was to it.

More was coming, and I knew it.

16

*A*nd here's some strange news, Doug wrote, *that I forgot to mention when we talked at New Year's. Bella has become a vegetarian. She and some other Tri Delts made up their minds never again to eat anything that had a face. They have their own table in the sorority house, and they call themselves The Vicious Veggies—vicious because they're vegetarians with a vengeance. They won't date anyone who eats meat, fowl, or fish! So guess what yours truly has to live on? Pasta, mostly. I've got pasta coming out of my ears!*

Dad and Evie and I were riding back from a used-farm-equipment sale where we'd gotten a rotary mower we'd been looking for.

It was a dirty thing the farmer hadn't bothered to clean properly. Its big blades were crusted with dried grass and mud, but it would mow the big pastures over at Atlees' just fine once it was oiled and waxed and put in the shed until spring.

We kept everything at our place shipshape. Dad was best at appearance upkeep, and I helped him, but it was Evie who tackled anything mechanical. She was good at any kind of repair.

Evie always drove us anywhere we were going.

She was loosening the red scarf around her neck and laughing at Doug's letter, which Mom had told me to take with me and read to them.

"The way Doug loves red meat? This will test him!" she said.

"That girl's making mincemeat out of him," said Dad.

"Not mince*meat*," I said. "She's turning him into a vegetable."

"What's got into Doug?" Dad said. "Hell, in high school he'd love 'em and leave 'em. He never got led around by the nose by any gal."

"He's a goner, I guess," I said.

"If Angel told you tomorrow you couldn't eat anything with a face, would *you* listen?"

"She wouldn't tell me that."

"But what *if*?" he persisted.

"It depends. If it was for health reasons I *might*. You gave up real coffee for Mom."

"That's *right*!" Evie said. "And she doesn't have to know you take a thermos into The Paradise and fill it up coupla times a week."

"Coffee's different," said Dad. "Your mother's the only person thinks coffee's a killer."

"But the point is," I said, "you gave it up for her, same as Doug gave up fish and fowl and meat!"

"Your mother is my *wife*. I been married to her all these years. I wouldn't have made such a promise when we were just dating."

"Parr's got you." Evie laughed.

"What about you, Evie?" I asked.

"I already gave something up, but nobody's noticed."

"What'd you give up?"

"You tell me," said Evie. "I gave something up just yesterday."

"What?" I asked.

"What'd you give up, Evie?" Dad said.

"You don't know?"

"*I* don't know," I said.

"You been with me all day, and you still don't know?"

I thought about it for a second and then I hit my forehead with my palm. "Cigarettes!" I said. "You haven't had a cigarette all day!"

Evie laughed.

"She's got one behind her ear," said Dad.

"That's where it'll stay, too," said Evie.

"You *haven't* been smoking!" said Dad. "I'll be darned!"

"I gave it up at midnight last night."

"How come?" I said.

"I just did."

"Yeah, but on your own steam," Dad said.

Evie didn't say anything.

"That's different," Dad said.

I was thinking: Patsy Duff must have been back at private school about two weeks now.

"Nobody could get you to give up *anything*," Dad said.

"Don't be too sure," Evie said.

I jumped in with "Congratulations, Evie."

"Thanks, Parr."

Dad didn't let go of it. I think it was sheer stupidity that made him pursue it, just dumb stubbornness.

He said, "I'd like to know who on this earth could get *you* to stop smoking. Cord doesn't have any guts that way."

"No, he doesn't," Evie said.

"Whoever did it did you a favor," I said.

"I know it," said Evie.

"You read an article?" Dad again.

"No, I didn't, Dad. It doesn't matter *who*. I'm

just taking Parr's side of the argument. You give things up sometimes if there's good reason."

"There was good reason for three or four years and it didn't stop you smoking," said Dad.

"I guess now I found a better reason," said Evie, but she didn't say what it was.

Dad finally got silent.

I said, "Dad, I'll flip you for who cleans the mower."

"I'll do it," he said.

"Since when?"

"Since when what?" He sounded glum.

"Since when do you make it so easy for me?"

"Easy's better than hard," Dad said. "Why not make it easy if you can do it?"

"Oh!" I said. "A little philosophy on the way home."

"Snap up the offer while you can, Parr," said Evie.

We both chuckled but Dad was silent.

Evie said, "Have Angel over for some venison steak this weekend, Parr. We'll do a big dinner. I'll invite Cord, too."

"Angel'd bring one of her mother's pies, I bet," I said.

Evie'd been going a lot of places with Cord since Christmas. Movies. Bowling. She was in a better mood than I could remember in a long time.

I kept thinking about that Jane Doe mailbox over in King's Corners. I'd think about it, and then I'd knock it off because I didn't like mysteries I believed I'd never have the solution to. I might have come right out and asked Evie a time we'd been alone together if she knew why Patsy Duff would rent a box there, but I didn't want to get Mrs. Kidder in trouble.

"I like Angel," said Evie. "She's got Anna Banana beat by miles."

"It's easy to beat Anna Banana," I said.

"You know what I mean, Parr. Angel's great!"

"I just wish I could drive," I said. "I hate having to hitch a ride there and back. It cramps my style."

"It doesn't seem to," Evie said.

Dad still wasn't joining the conversation.

He was sitting next to me, staring out the window, twiddling his thumbs. His hands were so rough we could hear the thumbs going.

We finally pulled into our drive and started down the road just as it was getting dark.

Long lanes of smoky gray clouds were traveling past the top of the sinking sun. Pete and Gracie were running to meet the truck, barking greetings. The snowdrifts were piled up on both sides of us.

Dad pushed the ashtray back and looked inside, as though he expected to see some old butts in there, even though Evie always emptied it before we took off to go anywhere. Maybe he wanted to believe she'd been kidding. I didn't know what he was doing that for.

We were walking up toward the house when Dad suddenly reached over and gave a little tug on the red scarf Evie had around her neck.

"That new?" he asked. Then, before she answered, he added, "You didn't get that around here."

"No, it was given to me," said Evie.

"I never saw you wear it."

"She's been wearing it every day," I said.

"Since when?" he said.

Evie said, "Since Christmas."

"Oh," he said. "Uh-huh."

That was all.

Then we went inside.

17

We always made a big fuss on Valentine's Day, maybe because winter was so boring.

Dad always bought one of those big, red, heart-shaped chocolate boxes from the drugstore at King's Corners, along with a huge, mushy "To My Wife" card.

Mom and Evie and I made our valentines, and Mom decorated the table, put on the pink cloth, blew up some balloons, made heart-shaped cupcakes with red-and-white frosting, and put out red candles.

We invited Angel to dinner. Evie offered to drive her over to our place and back, but Mr. Kidder said he'd come get her after—Evie shouldn't have to do all the driving.

Evie kept insisting she wanted to do the driving, but Mr. Kidder wouldn't hear of it.

The trouble started about an hour before it was time for Evie to leave for the drive to Floodtown.

I'd shown everyone the valentine I'd made for Angel, with the promise they wouldn't read what I'd printed inside.

"Is it a love poem?" Dad asked.

"It's not a poem. Never mind."

"I wrote your mother poems," he said.

"Those days are gone forever," Mom said. "Now Hallmark writes them for you."

Mom had finished setting the table, and called up to Evie that she was coming up to shower before dinner.

Evie yelled back, "Me first. I'll be fast."

We all had our valentines out on the table except for Evie, who hadn't brought hers downstairs yet.

I'd gotten one from Toni Atlee in Florida saying

she didn't miss anything about Duffton, including me, signed "Love and kisses, T."

Cord was off in Kansas City going to some lecture sponsored by Reed Joseph International, bird and predator control experts. We were trying to get rid of the pigeons and starlings on our land, because they caused hog disease.

Mom told Dad the timer was set for the casserole in the oven, and to pull it out when it dinged.

We went upstairs together. I wanted to show her the locket I'd picked out for Angel before I wrapped it. I hoped she'd offer to wrap it and she did, but we couldn't find any scissors.

She went to Evie's room to look for them and I heard her say, "What's this?"

Then I heard Evie charge out of the bathroom and say, "Are you in my room?"

"I was looking for a scissors and I couldn't help noticing—"

"Give me that!" Evie said.

"It was right out in the open on your bed, Evie! Who's Jane Doe?"

"It's a package I picked up for someone."

"It's open."

"I know it's open! Mom, here are the scissors. Just let me have some privacy."

"But who's Jane Doe, honey?"

"It's me. Okay?"

"I *see* the return address," said Mom. "Appleman School."

"So now you know. . . . I'm forced to sneak around to spare your feelings."

"I don't want you sneaking around, Evie. Don't do that for me."

"Really? You want to hear about it?"

There was a pause and then Mom said, "Maybe not."

"You bet not!" said Evie. "I didn't think you did."

"If you want to talk about it, I do."

"All right, Mother. This is a Valentine's gift from Patty. It's an ID bracelet, and there's also some k. d. lang tapes in the box."

"Why is it addressed to Jane Doe?"

"I've got a P.O. box over at King's Corners in that name. I didn't want to chance getting mail at the Duffton post office, even under a false name."

"So you two have been writing each other all along."

"I mail my letters from King's Corners, no return address, just in case her father's got the school on the lookout for anything with my name on it mailed from here. . . . I'm eighteen years old and I have to sneak around."

I could hear Mom sigh, and the bedsprings squeak as someone sat down.

"Evie," Mom said, "I wasn't born yesterday. I'm not unfamiliar with lesbianism. Gays. Whatever you call it. Is that what you claim you are?"

"It's not what I claim I am. It's what I am."

"You don't know that for sure, honey."

"I know it. For sure. I've always known it. I just never met anyone like me."

"*She* did this to you."

"She didn't do anything to me, and I didn't do anything to her. Did Angel do anything to Parr to make him fall in love at first sight?"

"That's different."

"Did Parr do anything to Angel? Didn't it just happen?"

"I'm not going to get into an argument with you, Evie. I'm going to tell you what I think. If this is *true*, if you really are what you say you are, all the more reason for trying to fix yourself up a little. Be more presentable. Be a little more feminine."

"Patty likes me the way I am. She likes me in pants, with my hair slicked back, in my bomber jacket—"

"Your *brother's* bomber jacket."

"Okay. She likes me in my brother's bomber

jacket, and she likes me taking long steps, sinking my hands in my pockets, and all the other stuff you say I shouldn't do. The only thing she didn't like was my smoking. The only reason she didn't like my smoking was because it isn't good for my health. So I gave it up!"

Mom was silent.

Then Evie said, "Some of us *look* it, Mom! I know you so-called normal people would like it better if we looked as much like all of you as possible, but some of us don't, can't, and never will! And some others of us go for the ones who don't, can't, and never will."

Mom didn't answer.

Then Evie said, "There's nothing to cry about!"

"I'm not crying for myself. I'm crying for you, honey."

"I'm trying to tell you save your tears, Mom. For the first time in my life someone likes me just the way I am."

Another silence.

"*Loves* me," Evie added. "Mom, look at this bracelet. See what's engraved here."

"I can't, Evie," Mom answered. "Not now. . . . I have to shower. I have to get ready. I can't deal with this now. You have to get Angel, too."

"And after dinner I have to go somewhere, Mom.

I was going to take Angel home and call you from the road. Lie and say the Pontiac broke down. But the truth is I'll be gone overnight. I'm meeting Patty tomorrow. We're having lunch over near Appleman."

I heard the bedsprings creak again, heard Mom say, "Don't tell your father this, Evie. I'll call Mr. Kidder and say you're going somewhere anyway. Then you do what you'd planned on doing."

"Lie," Evie said.

"Yes. Lie."

Angel's Valentine gift to me was a wash-off tattoo of an angel flying through clouds. She'd made me a card drawn with a heart, our initials inside, pierced by an arrow.

Before I could stop her she'd read aloud what I'd written inside my card: *I love everything about you!*

"Now you're talking!" Dad rubbed his hands together, pleased.

Mom helped her put on my locket, and Dad said now he supposed Angel wanted his picture to put in there.

We laughed a lot. Angel was right at home with

my folks, as they were with her.

I felt sorry for Evie, even though she seemed to be in a great mood. I kept remembering hearing her ask Mom to look at the ID bracelet Patsy gave her, and Mom saying she couldn't.

Angel had to be back by ten o'clock, which was just when Cord surprised us by showing up with candy and a card for Evie. He'd skipped the last half of the lecture so he could make an appearance. He was having a cup of coffee with us when Dad answered the phone and told us all the fan belt gave out on Evie's car and she was going to stay over at the Twin Oaks motel.

Cord said, "I thought Evie always had an extra fan belt in her trunk."

"Seems she doesn't."

"Tell you what. I'll go get her. I got to go back over that way tomorrow, anyway."

"After all the driving you did today?" Mom said. "I won't hear of it!"

"I asked her why she didn't just go back to the Kidders'," said Dad, "but she said there wasn't room there and she didn't want to wake them up."

"I'll go get her," Cord said. "You can't give a gal a valentine on the fifteenth of February."

"She's probably already in bed," said Mom.

"Let him go," said Dad. "I never can sleep away

from home, and I bet Evie can't, either."

Mom followed Cord out the door, spoke to him, came back looking worried.

We were all in bed when the phone rang the second time. I wasn't asleep and I bet Mom couldn't sleep, either, but Dad got awakened and cussed his way downstairs saying who was *that* calling up at midnight?

Then he yelled up to Mom, "Evie's not there. Cord says should he call up the Kidders at this hour?"

"No!" said Mom. She'd gotten out of bed and was just outside my door.

"Well, where the heck is she? Twin Oaks doesn't know anything about it!"

"Tell Cord to come back to Duffton," Mom said.

"Maybe she's trying to get a ride somewhere on the road," said Dad. Then I heard him tell Cord, "Did you take a look by the Texaco station down at the turn to King's Corners? There's a phone booth—"

Mom interrupted. "Tell Cord to come home, Douglas."

"But why? He's already there. He might as well look around for her. He maybe *ought* to call the Kidders."

"I know where Evie is," said Mom. "I told Cord she wasn't there, but he wouldn't believe it."

"Because she *is* there, somewhere!"

"Tell Cord to come back, then hang up."

"*I* spoke to her, Cynnie, and she said she was—"

"Do as I say, Douglas! Evie didn't have car trouble."

My father came back up the stairs, shouting, "What is this about? Where is Evie?"

"I expect she's gone on to Jefferson City!"

"Jefferson City?"

"Don't get Parr out of bed now. Come on in and I'll tell you about it."

Their bedroom door slammed.

I couldn't hear her clearly after that, but I could hear him.

I could hear "loan." I could hear "Duff." I could hear "Patsy," "Evie," and a whole lot of other words my dad wasn't known for saying inside our house.

19

By the end of February Cord and Evie had had a showdown, so Cord knew what was going on between Evie and Patsy.

He acted like it was a big joke. Once, when he'd gone to St. Luke's with us and we were all saying The

Lord's Prayer, he said in this loud voice, "Deliver us from Evie," instead of "Deliver us from evil," and he laughed and nudged Evie, who gave him a sharp elbow in his ribs, her face flushed for a moment.

Dad was heartbroken, I think. This was an Evie he didn't know, and the two of them together were always on edge. It got worse in March, when Mom went down to Little Rock to visit her folks. Every year at that time she spent a few days at the Parrs', but this year it seemed longer because of what was going on between Evie and Dad.

One Sunday Evie came down to breakfast in new navy-blue pants, a new navy-blue cashmere jacket, and a white shirt open at the neck. Her hair was slicked back and she had the red scarf around her neck.

Dad said, "I won't be going to church with you, Evie."

"Since when do you miss church?"

"I got work to do."

"Why don't you relax? You *got* the loan."

"No thanks to you," he said.

Evie got herself some coffee and sat down at the table with us.

"Is she buying you clothes now?" Dad asked her.

"I got a birthday coming, remember. So we went shopping yesterday."

Evie'd been going to Jefferson City every Friday

night for weeks. She'd come back late Saturday night.

According to Evie, Patsy Duff would meet her for lunch on Saturday, they'd go to a movie, then Evie'd drive home.

Dad never talked any of it through with Evie, but he made cracks, and he kept his distance from her. In fact, if he could help it he didn't spend any time alone with her.

I knew he wished he could control her or throw her out of the house, but he needed her too much. I heard him complain to Mom they were sitting on a tinderbox—it was just a matter of time before Mr. Duff got wind of it.

Mom just kept saying, "They aren't *doing* anything, Douglas."

He'd say back, "We don't know what they're doing and not doing!"

Evie didn't let up on him that Sunday morning.

She said, "Come on and go to church, Dad. This is the Sunday Parr's going to The Church of the Heavenly Spirit, remember."

"You don't need to say *remember* after everything you say. I'm not dotty yet, despite your shenanigans."

"I'll be all alone in our pew," said Evie.

"You made your bed," Dad said. "Anyway, it's going to rain cats and dogs. I got to get a fence in before it does."

"Do you know how you can tell if it's rained cats and dogs?" Evie asked.

"No and I don't care," Dad said.

"How can you tell?" I asked her.

"You step in a poodle," said Evie, grinning.

I laughed but Dad just grunted and got up from the table. He took his cup and plate over to the sink.

He said, "Parr? Are you having dinner with the Kidders?"

I said I was and he said to call him when I was ready to come home.

Then he said, "You're too dressed up for church, Evie, if you know what I mean."

"What *do* you mean?" she said.

"Those aren't farm clothes, they're serious clothes. Be different if it was Doug wearing them home from college."

He left the room before Evie could answer.

I was used to talking with her about Patsy Duff. We never got on the subject of homosexuality, or even how they felt about each other, but she'd tell me things Patsy'd say and stuff they did together.

Patsy was teaching her to dance, teaching her a little French, getting her to eat things she'd never tasted like calamari and steamed mussels.

On the way to Floodtown she asked me if I

thought her clothes were "too much."

"I wouldn't mind having them," I said. I felt the buttery texture of her jacket with my thumb and first finger. "They even *feel* rich."

"Maybe Dad's right and I shouldn't wear them to church."

"Wear what you want to wear," I said.

"Patty spent a fortune on them!"

"She's got it to spend."

"That's what Patty says. She says, 'Don't deny me the pleasure of giving you something great—that's what money's for!'"

"I don't know if Mr. Duff would think that's what his money's for."

"Patty's got her own money. Her grandmother Duff left her a trust fund."

"Lucky her," I said.

"Are you being sarcastic, Parr?"

"No, I'm being bitter. I wish I was rich."

"Because I want you to like her. She's really neat!"

"I don't dislike her," I said. "I don't know her well enough to like her."

We passed the Vets' Memorial Statue and saw a bra hanging from the bayonet.

"They're so original in this town," Evie said.

I said, "When Doug was home last weekend there was a huge pair of men's jockey shorts there, and he got ticked off and he said he hated this town. Figure that out."

"Anna Banana is getting to him. It's not Duffton getting to him. It's her."

"Gawd, I hope not! I don't want to be left holding the bag. What will we do if Doug decides he's not going to farm?"

"Don't say 'we,' Parr. I'm not dead set on hanging around here anymore, either."

I just sat there as though something heavy had fallen on me and was holding me down.

Evie said, "Sorry to say it, little brother, but that's how I feel."

I said, "You'll change your mind," but it was only wishful thinking. The whole idea of Evie in the same sentence with change, once she was set on her course, was what you call an oxymoron. Opposite ideas combined.

20

The Church of the Heavenly Spirit was celebrating its new building. It was one large room with a pulpit and cross at the front, and choir loft in the rear.

Angel was singing a solo that morning, so she didn't sit with the congregation.

I sat between her mother and father.

Pastor Bob preached this fiery sermon on the sin of envy, followed by Angel's voice.

When she began singing, I couldn't imagine what the hymn was all about.

The first verse was:

C-L-O-C-K—*"The world is like a shelf,*
Do you ever think You should be like myself?
For I tick, tick, quick, quick,
With a merry chime working all the time.
Tick!" said the clock;
"What?" said I.
"You can learn a lesson from my tick, if you try."

I sat there thinking about what Evie'd just told me. Dad and Cord had decided on expanding our hog operation, and planting only corn come spring. I'd heard them say that with Evie full-time and me part-time they'd only need a few hands extra; then in summer Doug would be back, and we'd all pitch in and manage for three months ourselves.

Then after that what?

Dad would lose heart if he thought that in the

future there'd be no Doug, and no Evie, either.

He'd already told me he didn't want me to be a farmer, not if it wasn't in me. He'd said I should go to the university and spend my first two years thinking about a major. Maybe business, he said. Maybe even advertising, since the journalism school taught it, and I always had a lot to say about the commercials on TV.

I liked the idea of making up commercials. I figured I could come up with better ideas than most I saw on the tube. It was something I'd never thought about before, and I'd even told Angel I was giving some thought to being an advertising man.

But I knew I'd never be able to walk away from the farm if both Doug and Evie did.

For the first time the thing between Evie and Patsy Duff got to me. If it hadn't been for Patsy, my sister might have gone along without ever thinking she was all that different. She'd managed all right before Patsy came into her life. . . . Now Patsy was luring her with expensive clothes, teaching her dance steps (*where* was that going on?), and introducing her to all sorts of sophisticated things Evie could have easily died without ever missing.

It seemed to me very possible that a Duff would be responsible for me never even getting to the University of Missouri. That made me damn mad, too, that it was a Duff doing me in. Lately we were always in deep shit because of that family.

I'd never be able to walk away from the farm, probably.

It'd be on my conscience.

Then like God was reading my mind, Angel's voice rang out loud and clear on the last verse.

> C-L-O-C-K—"And I've a loud alarm;
> Conscience says Wake up! Sin wants to do you harm!
> Keep awake! wake! wake! wake!
> With a merry chime working all the time.
> Tick!" said the clock;
> "What?" said I;
> "You can learn a lesson from my 'larm, if you try."

That night I woke up in a cold sweat from a nightmare.

Evie was being buried over in Duffton Cemetery.

Patsy Duff was standing there weeping, holding a smoking gun.

21

"Y ou never had a beer?" said Cord. "Not one?"

"I've had a taste," I told him. "It didn't thrill me."

"It's an *acquired* taste, Parr. Like those oysters Patsy Duff's got Evie swallowing. You heard about that?"

"I didn't hear oysters."

"Yeah, oysters! Yuck!"

It was the week of Easter vacation, and I'd gone over to King's Corners with him, the mower we'd bought at the farm sale last winter loaded in back.

It needed repair, turned out, and Evie'd given up on it.

We were sitting in the rear of the pickup with our feet dangling, taking in the sun of an afternoon like summer smack in the middle of April.

Cord was holding an empty beer can, crushing it with his fingers, tossing it into the bin behind Howell Hardware, a favorite parking place for the farm trucks.

He plucked another can from a six-pack and said, "Here's yours. Try it. It'll cheer you up."

I took it.

I told him my worst fears about Doug and Evie leaving the farm on my hands.

"Evie could have fixed that mower, too," Cord said.

"Probably."

"Evie could fix a space shuttle if she put her mind to it. She knows machinery like she knows soil. It's in her blood."

"Or was," I said.

"That thing's not going to last, Parr. You think a girl like Patsy Duff's going to want Evie once she's met herself a man? Thing is, those girls go to private school don't have the opportunity to find out what the male sex is all about. They keep them like nuns at those places."

"Patsy used to date Ned Thacker."

"He's just a kid! He's a preppie. He's not a man!"

"I don't know anything about it," I said.

"That's why I'm telling you about it. Now Evie's got her man's ways, for sure, but a lot of women from the farm do, because they do men's work. She'd have snapped out of it if this thing hadn't gotten blown all out of proportion."

"That's what I think. It's Patsy's fault."

"She turned Evie around, next thing she'll take a walk."

"I hope so."

"I know so. . . . What do *they* do together? Two females! Hah!"

"I don't know what they do together."

"Not much."

"I don't even know what two guys do together."

I knew. I'd learned about it in health and nutrition, and nothing to do with sex is all that mysterious to a farm boy. I guess what I meant was I couldn't figure out two guys feeling that way.

"Two guys get AIDS together," said Cord.

He was fooling with a thick, black perma-marker he'd used to make a sign advertising the pickup for sale. We'd fixed it up in the window behind the gun rack, hoping to attract a buyer. Cord had his eye on a secondhand Dodge with a larger truck bed.

He was making a big black heart, with EVIE LOVES PATSY inside it, on a hunk of cardboard.

"Do you think being a dyke is sinful?" I asked him.

"*Hell* no! It's not serious enough to be a sin. It's kid stuff. Two women is . . . Now two men—that's another matter. That's sin in the Bible."

"What are you doing *that* for?" I looked at the black heart he was drawing with their names inside.

"I'm fooling around. I had to take the whole afternoon off because of them, didn't I? Patsy could have fixed that mower."

"You mean Evie."

"Did I say Patsy? I'd like to fix *her* mower."

"I thought it was my sister you liked."

"I do like Evie. I even love her. But Evie's what I'd choose for my wife. Patsy's another story. I'd like to *change* that little gal."

"You'd like to go to an early grave," I said. "Duff would kill you with his bare hands."

"Don't I know it! But I can dream, can't I, Parr?"

He was right about the beer.

I didn't mind the taste so much after a whole can, and I had a second one when he passed it to me.

I felt a little guilty that we'd left all the work to Dad, Evie, and two hired hands, but Cord was right: We wouldn't even have been there if Evie'd put her mind back on repairing stuff. She didn't seem to do anything extra anymore, the way she used to like to tinker with the tractors, the planters, the bailers and harrows. She listened to a lot of music up in her room, and wrote a lot of letters and "statements" in her notebook.

"Do you still think of marrying Evie?" I asked him.

"I plan to, Parr."

"I'm not so sure she'll want to do that," I said.

"Isn't that what you want? Me and her to marry?"

"*I'd* like it fine, but Evie's all different now."

"She's not different. Clothes do not make the man." Cord laughed. "She's still Evie. We just got to get her past this stage she's in."

"Huh?" I said. "*We* have to get her past it?"

"With the help of old man Duff," said Cord. He opened himself another can of beer and slung an arm around my shoulders. "I have never been an idle fellow, Parr. Did you know that about me?"

"What's that supposed to mean?" I had a gulp of beer.

"I may be a dropout, may not have the education Doug has or the smarts you have, but my mind"—he tapped his forehead with his fingers—"is always busy, Parr."

"Glaaad to hear it," I crowed. "Glaaad to hear it!"

"A little beer goes a long way with you, buddy."

"Yeah, well, isn't that what it's for?"

"Drink up. See if you can chug-a-lug. Can you chug-a-lug?"

"Do bears crap in the woods?" I said. I tipped the can up and swallowed.

Cord clapped.

He said, "You're all right, Parr!"

He passed me another.

He said, "I've got a little plan, Parr. You know what happens tonight?"

"What happens tonight?" I laughed. I felt good.

"Tonight old man Duff brings his little dyke princess home from boarding school for her Easter vacation. I heard him telling someone that down at the P.O. this morning."

"Whoopee," I said.

"Yeah, whoopee. . . . Now I was wondering what he'd think if he was driving her past the Vets' Memorial, which is right under that big old street-light, and he saw a sign hanging off the bayonet that said this."

He held up the black heart with EVIE LOVES PATSY printed inside it.

I said, "And vice versa," because why put the blame on Evie?

"Oh, that's good, Parr. That's good."

He took the marker out of his shirt pocket and added AND VICE VERSA.

Then he got another idea, slapped his knee and laughed, and underlined VICE.

"How about *that*?" he said.

"He'll croak if he sees that," I said.

"He'll see it all right," said Cord. "Who doesn't look to see what's on that bayonet every time he goes by there?"

"Everybody looks," I said.

"That's right, Parr. And we're not doing this *to*

Evie, either—we're doing it *for* Evie. The only way she's going to snap out of this thing is for old man Duff to get that dyke daughter of his out of Evie's way. If I know him, he'll send her east, put her in some New England boarding school."

"School's almost out."

"He'll send her to some camp, send her to relatives, send her somewhere Evie can't get to her. You'll see."

"Evie'd go right after her, Cord."

"With what? She don't have a plugged nickel, Parr!"

"She's got savings. She never spent a dime all her life until this happened!"

"She can't match Duff money, or outsmart him. Let Duff handle this. You'll see. When we get to Duffton, one of us is going to jump out and stick it up there, and one of us is going to be the lookout."

"In broad daylight?"

"Guys stick things up there all the time in broad daylight and never get caught. It's only going to take a second."

I said I'd be the lookout.

"You're not a licensed driver, Parr. If we need to get away fast, *I* got to be behind the wheel."

I don't think I'd have agreed to do it if I hadn't had

the beers. But the one night Doug ever got drunk in high school and hanged the principal in effigy from the County High flagpole, Mom said not to blame the liquor, there was malice behind the act. She said maybe the whiskey gave Doug the nerve, but he'd always had it in for Mr. Friar.

Time hadn't made me a big fan of Patsy Duff's, but I didn't think I had it in for Evie.

Still, it was Evie letting me down: no warning, nothing. *Sorry to say it, little brother, but you're stuck here forever.*

22

Evie was in the tractor down on the Atlee land, chiseling the field from north to south and back again. Dad was doing the same thing on our bottom-land.

Next day Doug would be home to help knife in the fertilizer, as we got ready to plant.

I could smell the newly turned ribbons of earth all through the air. There was nothing like that smell. I stood there taking it in, worrying about another smell: the beer on my breath.

Lucky for me, Mom was over at the sheds receiving a delivery on the seed corn.

I went up to the house and showered and gargled with Listerine. I opened the window to let the steam out. No one had to know I'd sobered myself up under the hot water.

I was towel drying my hair as I passed Evie's room. I saw a framed photograph on Evie's bureau. That was new. I stepped inside her room and looked at Patsy Duff's smiling face, trying to hate it so I wouldn't feel the regret beginning to seep through me for putting that sign up on the bayonet at the Vets' Memorial.

The red scarf was draped over the mirror. The ID bracelet was sitting in a glass ashtray Evie now used for her school ring and change.

I looked at the bracelet. It had EVIE engraved on the front. On the back there was PATTY, and in smaller letters: *Our love . . . it just keeps rolling.*

I figured Evie'd said something to her about the river, same as she'd said to me that you couldn't change Patty—she was like the river. I remembered the song: "Old man river . . . he just keeps rolling."

When the phone rang, I had to run downstairs to answer it, since our only extension was in the barn.

Angel said, "Parr? It's me. Can you talk?"

"Cat doesn't have my tongue," I said. "How are you, honey?"

"No, I mean, is your family right there?"

"No one's here. What's the matter?"

"I'm not home. I am at a pay phone, so can you call me back?"

She gave me the number and I pushed the buttons.

"What's the matter? You okay?"

"Parr, there's all kinds of talk about your sister. Mom came home from Barker's store filled with it. Parr, they're saying she's a lezzie and there's a sign about it over at the memorial statue in Duffton."

"What kind of sign?" I said, all innocence. But that was something I'd never thought about: Angel and her family hearing that kind of rumor.

"They're saying she's after Mr. Duff's daughter, Parr!"

"I'll be coming over to your place tonight," I said. "We can talk about it."

"Mama doesn't want her driving you over here, Parr."

"Huh? What difference does it make if Evie gives me a ride?"

"Mama says Daddy won't want her around here. We're having to redo our mortgage, and Mama says Mr. Duff could hurt us, Parr. . . . Parr, does your sister *know* there's a sign up about her?"

"No, she doesn't know."

"Do your folks know what they're saying about Evie?"

"It probably won't come as a surprise," I said.

"It's a surprise to us! It's a shock is what it is! Mama asked me if she ever tried anything with me."

"Come *on*! Your mama said that?"

"And Mama said she *does* wear men's clothes."

"She works on a farm! What's she going to wear?"

"She didn't mean her work clothes, Parr. Mama said she's the one who gets mail from that box Patsy Duff rented, and when she comes in for it, she's got on a man's jacket."

News traveled like lightning in a small town. Cord and I had only made one stop in Duffton after we stuck that thing on the bayonet. It hadn't been up there but a few hours.

I said, "I'll get somebody else to drive me over tonight." I wondered who that would be. I could always get Evie to take us anywhere, no matter how hard she worked all day. She'd say, "What I do for love!" and drive not glancing at us, because she knew there weren't a lot of times we could kiss or even touch, certainly not around Angel's father, who'd drive us places with one eye on the road and one eye on us.

Dad would be too tired when he ever did get in

from the fields, and he'd be in the office studying the futures figures with Mom. They always went over the prices when we were getting ready to plant.

"Parr?" Angel said. "Don't come tonight. I got homework, anyway."

"It's Easter vacation, Angel!"

"I got Bible school homework, honey. Mama says I haven't been paying enough attention to church."

"Because of *this*? Is that why she said that?"

"I think so. . . . Evie isn't one, is she, Parr?"

"Would you care if she was, Angel?"

"I'd be afraid, Parr."

"Of *Evie*?"

"Well, not of Evie . . . of what she was, if she was one."

"You got more sense than that, Angel!"

"She's supposed to be after Mr. Duff's daughter."

"Did the sign *say* that? I bet it didn't say that!"

"I didn't see the sign."

"I don't think it said that."

"I only know what they're saying at Barker's."

"Is your mother telling people about the P.O. box?"

"Of course not! That's government property. She wouldn't tell who had a box there. She just told us."

"I'll try to get over there tomorrow," I said. "I don't know how, because we're planting tomorrow."

"It's better to wait, Parr."

"Wait till when?"

"I'll call you. . . . I don't know how Daddy's going to take this. You didn't tell me if she was or wasn't, Parr."

"Of course she's not!" I lied.

"I hope not," said Angel. "I got to go now, Parr. I'll call you."

"Love you, Angel."

"Love you, too. 'Bye!"

I dialed Cord's number and didn't get an answer.

I knew, anyway, it was too late to get that sign down.

The damage was done.

23

I wished I had a place to go that night.

I sat around watching TV, watching Evie sit around waiting for the phone to ring. I knew that was what she was doing. She kept looking at her watch, pacing, opening Cokes, and eating a lot of licorice candy, which she claimed helped take away the nicotine craving.

After Mom and Dad finished in the office, Dad went up to bed and Mom started baking.

She always made a lot of cookies for Doug when he came home, and for all of us busy with the planting.

She noticed Evie was downstairs, and she knew why, too. Evie was expecting a call, and she wanted to be the one who grabbed the phone when it rang.

"Is Patsy expected tonight?" she asked Evie.

"Yes."

"I thought so."

"You were right."

Evie was reading the Ruth Rendell mystery Cord had given her for Christmas, but she wasn't turning the pages very fast.

"Do you think she's going to call here?" Mom asked Evie.

"I know she is. It's early, though."

"It's ten o'clock," said Mom.

"She'll probably be another hour. They were going to have dinner on the way."

"Patsy and Mr. Duff?"

"That's right."

"Mrs. Duff, too?"

"No. She's busy with her gin bottle."

"That's not kind, Evie."

"*She's* not kind. She doesn't give a damn."

"Maybe that's why Patsy's the way she is," Mom said. "Poor child."

"Patty's not a poor child. She's a survivor. And she's not the way she is, quote unquote, because of her mother's drinking."

"You don't know that," said Mom.

"Do you think I'm the way I am because of something you and Dad did?"

"I don't think it helped that your father got you all interested in repairing tractors and doing other male things. Just because Doug wasn't good at that kind of work didn't mean you had to take it on."

"Oh, Mom, get real," said Evie. "I came out of the womb ready to handle tools. I knew how to change a tire when I was six, and when I was ten I could fix anything broken. You couldn't have learned it if Dad had spent an hour every day of the week instructing you!"

"Too bad you forgot," I said. "You could have fixed the mower and saved Cord and me a trip today." Saved your own neck, too, I thought, because I was looking for something to blame that damn sign on besides myself.

"Don't count on me so much," said Evie. "Not anymore don't."

"Meaning what?" My mother looked up at that remark.

"I've been thinking about living somewhere else."

"Where would that be, Evie?"

"New York. San Francisco. A big city, instead of a hick town."

"And what would you do?" said my mother.

"Get a job and work my way through college. I'd like to learn computers."

"Well, you're good with ours. I don't know half of what you know about ours," said Mom. I figured she was handling the whole idea in her usual way: not showing she was upset, playing along with whatever Evie said.

"*Ours,*" Evie scoffed. "Ours is old hat! Patty's got a laptop you can send a fax on."

"Patty, Patty, Patty," said Mom.

"Or Angel, Angel, Angel, when it's Parr doing the talking," said Evie.

Mom looked at me. "And what happened with your date tonight, Parr?"

"Angel's got Bible school homework."

"One thing I was wrong about," said Mom. "The Kidders aren't holy rollers at all. The Church of the Heavenly Spirit is probably much like St. Luke's. Right, Parr?"

"The hymns are different."

"Oh, well, the hymns are different in the various denominations. That's not a great difference."

"They talk about sin a lot, too," I said.

"I think they're a little more rigid than we are."

"Yeah," I said. "I think so."

"But you'd never know it from Angel," said Evie. "She's not uptight."

Just wait, I thought.

And it was the waiting that was getting to me, the thought of what was happening probably right about then as Mr. Duff drove past the statue, the waiting for the shit to hit the fan.

But Evie was still sitting down in our parlor at midnight, and I don't know how many hours past.

The phone never rang.

24

Every morning around five thirty I got up to use the bathroom, then went back to bed for a half hour. The roosters across the way would be getting up about the same time, and I'd hear them crowing. The sky would be changing from dark blue to light blue.

I saw Evie's bed still made, went halfway down the stairs, and saw her sleeping on the couch in her clothes.

In thirty minutes the clock radio would wake up my folks with the farm report and the day's prices.

We had a squeaky mailbox down on the road in front of our house. When it was a quiet day, we could hear the mailman open and shut it.

That's what I heard as I was starting back to bed. I knew it couldn't be any mailman, not at that hour, so I went to the window and looked out in the time to see one of the Duffarm station wagons head down the road. Their wagons were all long white Buick Roadmasters—you couldn't miss them.

I pulled on my pants and slipped into my loafers, colliding with Dad as I went out into the hall.

"Did you see that? Someone from Duffarm put something in our box."

"What are you doing up?" I said.

"I wake up early on planting days. You know that."

We went downstairs together.

Dad put his finger to his lips in a *shhhh* gesture when he saw Evie on the couch.

Dad was in jeans, buttoning his shirt, brushing his hand through his hair as we headed out the door.

"You don't have to come. Make some coffee. I'll get it," he said.

"I'll come."

"You don't even have a shirt on!"

"I don't need one."

"Curiosity killed the cat," he said.

My heart felt like it'd come through my skin. I was out of breath from it.

"What in the hell does Duff *want*?" Dad said.

I said, "Who knows?" But I knew the chickens were coming home to roost now and I was sick inside for what I'd done to my sister.

"It hasn't got to do with Evie, anyway," Dad said. "She's right there on the couch. . . . What's she doing there? Was she out last night?"

"No. Where would she go?"

"That *girl's* home, isn't she?"

"I don't know."

"We're going to make real coffee before your mother gets up. I got a pound yesterday. I'm not planting on decaf. . . . She won't even know."

"When's Doug due?"

"He'll be here for dinner."

That meant noon. We ate dinner at noon days we planted.

Dad opened the box. He had to yank the cardboard out. There was a piece of paper clipped to it.

He looked at the sign and said, "Damn!"

My teeth began to chatter. Not from the cold. From fear. Not of Dad. Not even of Duff. But fear of what had gotten into me, and I don't mean the beer.

"You see this sign?"

I looked at it. I felt like puking.

"What the hell is this about?"

Then he read the paper.

He read it aloud.

"Douglas, I took this sign off the Vets' statue last night! I am going to see Sheriff Starr about Evie. You don't seem to be able to do anything about her! She may need to told by someone in authority that Patsy is a minor. Thanks to Evie, we have a disgrace on our hands! Everyone in Duffton saw this thing! No more polite warnings, tell her! I mean business now!

G.K.D."

Dad took a deep breath.

I said, "What's Sheriff Starr supposed to do, arrest Evie? You can't arrest someone for having a crush on someone, can you?"

"Don't call it a crush. We know it's no crush."

"Still, what's Sheriff Starr supposed to do?" Could he actually *do* something to Evie?

"It's not the sheriff I'm afraid of. Duff can make plenty of trouble, Parr, and you know it."

"Yeah, I know it." I knew it. Finally. And I knew Evie was the one Duff would get.

"Now listen to me, Parr. Evie's not to know about

this right away. First things first, understand? We got to get the seed down first."

Dad rolled the cardboard up and stuck the note from Duff in his back pocket. We headed back toward the house.

"Your mother's got the light on now, so she heard, too. We're going to tell her he's having a sale. Tell her he's selling off some old equipment and putting notices in mailboxes. Remember, he did that last year, sold off those tractors."

"Okay," I said. "She'll want to see the notice."

"Not if I say I left it in the barn. I'm going down there now. You try to get the coffee brewing before she gets downstairs. There's a bag of it in my bottom desk drawer."

"I'll never make it. She's probably heading downstairs right now."

"You suggest we have real brewed coffee because of the planting. Sometimes she listens to you kids."

"Okay."

"If I ever find out who did this, I'll kill 'em."

"Yessir," I said, my stomach turning over.

"Who's even seen 'em together in Dufftown? They haven't been hanging around here!"

"No, they haven't," I said. He didn't know about the P.O. box in King's Corners. Mom spared him a lot of details.

"Remember, not one word to Evie, Parr." Then he added something that made me want to die. "I know you're close to her, know you probably take her side in this thing, but now it's way past taking sides."

I couldn't answer him.

He said, "When you get inside, you start babbling about the coffee. Tell your mother it was just a notice of a sale, and then blah blah about the coffee. Hear?"

I nodded.

I did as I was told while Dad went down to the barn.

He figured right. Mom got into the coffee issue and didn't pay attention to the sale story.

Evie was upstairs taking a shower, getting ready to plant, said Mom.

"If he'd only have one cup, that'd be different," said Mom. "But he has two, sometimes three, and there's no sense getting his heart pumping at the crack of dawn."

"How about half and half?" I suggested.

"All *right*!" Mom laughed. "Half and half. He won't know the difference. You get the bag from his drawer and put it out here where he can see it."

"How'd you know where it was?"

"You think I don't know your father's hiding places?"

I was trying hard to keep up my end of the conversation when Cord's pickup pulled into the driveway.

"Good. Cord's right on time! Call him in for some coffee," said Mom.

After a while both Cord and Dad came inside.

"Have we got a great day or what!" Cord said.

"We couldn't ask better," said Dad. Then he gave me the eye, motioned me to follow him into the office.

"You two come back here and get some breakfast!" said Mom.

"We're coming, honey," Dad called sweetly over his shoulder, but when he turned around to face me, there was fire in his eyes.

"I know who did it!" he said. He was whispering at me, his words spitting out of him. "Don't say a thing now, Parr. I just solved the mystery!"

"How'd you do that?" I said.

"There's cardboard just like the stuff Duff sent over here in Cord's back window. Same cardboard, same black marker. Advertising his pickup for sale!"

I just stood there, my knees as weak as a newborn calf's.

"It figures!" Dad hissed. "That jackass tries to get his own way any way he can!"

25

"**A**ny messages?" Evie asked.

"Nothing," said Mom.

Dad and Cord were washing up.

I was finished, and helping Mom get the stew from the pot to plates.

We weren't going to wait for Doug.

We'd had a good morning. We'd done all the back fields, and Cord had started over at Atlees' already.

"They say she's not there," Evie said.

"She knows you're planting, doesn't she?"

"Yep. But she would have called, you'd think, say she was here."

"She's here, Evie. Don't worry. She's probably gone shopping. Maybe she's getting her Easter outfit."

"From around here? I don't *think* so." Evie chuckled.

"What are you going to wear to church?"

"One of Dad's suits, a necktie." Evie grinned, and my mother reached out with a mock punch at her chin. "Behave," she said. "Spare your father today, all right?"

"I spare him all the time," said Evie.

Cord appeared. "Who're you sparing what?"

He sat himself down at the table.

"Not you," she said.

"Not me is right. Not anything," he said.

"You're being such a help, Parr," said Mom. "I suppose you want me to drive you to Angel's tonight."

"Who can move after we finish here?" I said.

"Since when are you ever too tired to see Angel?" said Mom.

"I'll take you over," Evie said.

"I'm not going," I said. "She's singing at the sunrise service, anyway. She'll need her sleep."

"Who's taking you to that?" Mom said.

"I'll do it!" said Evie. "What I do for love!"

"I'm not going," I said. I was pretty sure I wasn't invited, and more sure I didn't want Evie driving me.

"You coming to church with us, honey?" Mom asked.

"I do every year."

"I wasn't going to make you do it," said Mom, "but I do like the idea of the whole family in church on Easter Sunday."

Dad came in and sat down at the table.

Cord said, "I hope I'm included in the family, Mrs. Burrman."

"Be delighted," said Mom.

"Don't you ever go to your own church?" Dad asked.

"Why, Douglas!" said Mom, "What a thing to say."

"Just curious why he doesn't ever go to his own."

"Because Evie's not there," said Cord.

"Not ever going to be there, either," said Evie.

"So I'll go where you are," Cord said.

"See how much he thinks of you, Evie?" Dad said, and there was an edge to his voice.

I said, "Who's going to start the bread around?"

Cord reached for the bread basket. "We did good today, Douglas," he boomed.

"So far," said Dad. "So far."

"I might not go to church tomorrow," said Evie.

"You wouldn't skip Easter, honey."

"If she doesn't want to go, don't force her," said Dad.

"Since when?" Mom said.

"I'd go if it was sunrise, like at The Church of the Heavenly Spirit," Evie said, "but we waste the better part of the day going to the eleven o'clock at St. Luke's."

"I agree," said Dad. "We might not even be finished."

"We'll be finished," said Cord.

"Why are you selling your pickup?" Dad asked him.

"I need a bigger truck bed. That thing's ten years old anyway."

"I saw your sign," Dad said.

I said, "Dad, pass me the butter." I gave him the eye when he did, as if to remind him he didn't want to get anything started yet.

He shot me back an appreciative wink. I knew he was dying to get at Cord. I knew when he did, I was going down the tubes with him.

"What are you going to get?" Evie asked Cord.

"I got my eye on the Dodge Ram."

"You'll get rooked if you buy it from Deigh Dodge."

"Private owner," Cord said.

Somehow Dad got through dinner without saying much more to Cord. Then we heard a car pull into the drive.

"Here's Doug now," said Mom.

"About time," Dad said.

Cord was stretching his neck to see out in the driveway. "It's not Doug," he said.

Evie pushed back her chair, her face brightening.

"It's not your girlfriend, either," Cord said.

"Cord," said my father, "I've had about enough."

"Enough of what?" Cord answered.

Dad didn't get to say enough of what.

Evie said, "It's Sheriff Starr. What's he want?"

26

Dad sent Cord back to the Atlee fields, saying Sheriff Starr was there on family business.

Everybody in Duffton knew him. He mostly took care of domestic disputes on the farms, and traffic violations on the roads and highways.

He was a large, redheaded fellow with freckles and tight curly red hair. I went to County with Spots Starr, his son, who got his nickname from the same kind of freckles. Spots was a big deal at CHS, a senior, a sports hero.

The Sheriff stood there blowing on the lenses of his dark glasses, wiping them with a Kleenex.

When he finished saying he'd come at Mr. Duff's request, explaining about the sign fixed to the bayonet, telling everybody what it'd said, Evie cussed.

"I don't believe there *was* a sign," she said. "I believe he's making that up."

"There was a sign," said Dad. "It's down to the barn. Mr. Duff put it in our mailbox early this morning."

"Now, I don't know who put that one up there," said the sheriff, "but—"

"I *do* know," said Dad. "Cord put it there. You can go out that door and look in the back window of his pickup and see the same kind of sign!"

"Well, there was another one stuck to Duff's Porsche this morning," Sheriff Starr said, "the one *she* drives when she's here. A nasty one."

"Isn't there some kind of law against that type of thing?"

"Douglas, I'd have to arrest half the kids in the county if there was. I'm not here about the *sign*."

Evie was gripping her hands, cracking her knuckles, scowling.

I got up to clear the table.

Mom looked defeated, sitting there with her hands in her lap, staring down at the table.

"Say your say," Dad said. "This isn't the best of times for us to stop what we're doing."

"I'm sorry, Evie. I'm supposed to warn you to stay away from Patsy Duff."

"Warn *her* to stay away from Evie!" Dad barked.

"Well, Duffy's doing that." That was what old man Duff's cronies called him.

"Far as I know," said Evie, "there's no law against two females seeing each other."

"I never heard there was, either," said the sheriff. "Look, now, I'm just doing my duty. Mr. Duff made a complaint and I'm following through on it. That's all."

"What am I supposed to do about that complaint?" said Evie.

"Stop seeing that girl!" said Dad.

Evie shook her head. "No way. If she wants to see me, I'll see her. It's a free country!"

Dad slapped his hand down on the table. "You did your job, Sheriff. Now we're getting back to work! . . . Evie?"

Evie got up. She said to the sheriff, "You finished with me?"

He shrugged his shoulders. "I had my say, Evie. What you do about it is your own business, I guess."

"I'm not going to do anything about it," said Evie, "besides break Cord Whittle's neck!"

She and Dad went out the door, leaving me at the sink and Mom just sitting there while the sheriff stood.

"I don't know what to say," said Mom.

"Look, Cynnie," said the sheriff, "I wouldn't even have thought twice about any signs if Duffy hadn't called me over to his place. Cord puts up a sign, then someone copies the idea and it spreads. What's got into Cord pulling a prank like that?"

"It was more than a prank. It was malicious."

"I agree. . . . I don't know if there's truth to it or not, but even if there is—" He shrugged again.

"Even if there is, *what*?" Mom said.

"Nothing."

"Patsy Duff *is* a minor."

"Yes, she is, but Evie's not selling Patsy Duff liquor or trying to marry her"—he gave a snort—"or registering her to vote. I mean, *what* law is Evie breaking that I'm supposed to do something about?"

Mom had tears in her eyes by then, one rolling down her cheek. The sheriff said, "Oh, now, don't take this hard."

"How'm I supposed to take it?" Mom reached in her pocket for a Kleenex.

"I'll tell you something. I don't even think this thing is important. I had an uncle who was funny, and you wouldn't meet a nicer fellow. He didn't bother anyone, and—"

"Evie's not *funny*," said my mother. "She's not some freak."

"Neither was my uncle Bob, Cynnie. I didn't mean he was a freak. He was more a fluke. All families got a fluke—if not right in front of them, way back. We even had a rooster out to our place once you couldn't get to go near the hens for love or money! It happens!"

Mom blew her nose.

She said, "Did you tell all this to Mr. Duff?"

"No, ma'am. I just said I'd look into it. Did you ever try to tell Duffy anything?" He laughed. "That young lady of his has always been a rebel. I don't know how many speeding tickets I've written for her. She's got a wild streak. She's about the only thing Duffy can't control, and it gets to him. That's what this is all about. She's going through a stage."

"And Evie?" Mom asked.

He shrugged and grinned. "Evie's what she is, and whatever that is, it hasn't bothered anyone before, has it?"

Mom didn't answer for a second. Then she said, "Will he try to do anything more about it?"

The sheriff shifted his weight from one foot to the other and socked one palm with his fist. He said, "Cynnie, don't worry about this anymore. Patsy's going back to Jeff City Monday, and when she's finished there, Duffy's packing her off to Europe. This whole thing's going to blow over."

So Cord was right, in the long run, I thought.

It was the short run we had to get past.

And living with it *I* had to get past.

After Sheriff Starr left, Mom said, "This is what I mean, Parr. This is exactly what I mean!"

"What're you talking about, Mom?"

"Someone like Evie gets all the blame. She's the funny one, the fluke . . . and Patsy Duff is just a rebel with a wild streak."

Then she shook her head and blew her nose again. "I suppose I understand why Cord did what he did. He's feeling desperate, probably doesn't even know it himself. It's hard to feel yourself losing someone you love. But it was such gratuitous cruelty. . . . And for it to be done to Evie, too. Evie doesn't have a mean bone in her body."

I almost blurted out right then and there that I was in on it along with Cord.

But I was too big a coward. I couldn't face Mom's knowing I was capable of doing something like that. I couldn't imagine answering to Dad, much less Evie. I had a feeling then that if there was any way I could work it, it'd be a secret I would keep all my life.

27

That Saturday night Dad was like a hornet that had been stepped on but not killed. He was beat and angry: at Cord for what we'd done, at Doug for not getting home until the planting was already down, and at Evie for refusing to say she'd stop seeing Patsy Duff.

He had a shower and a sandwich and then he went straight to bed.

Evie had a shower, too. Then she took off in her Pontiac, not saying where she was going.

Around nine o'clock Mr. Kidder called me to say he'd pick me up at five the next morning, so I could attend the sunrise service at The Church of the Heavenly Spirit.

Mom was good-natured about it, but when we got up to our room, Doug read me out.

"I broke my neck to get here so we could all go to St. Luke's together. You know how Mom likes that at Easter."

"You should have broke your neck to plant with us."

"I had an interview with the dean this morning. It was the only time he could see me, Parr. . . . I've got some news."

I thought, Uh-oh. I knew something was coming. I knew my brother. He'd dismissed the Evie thing by saying there was no point talking about it: What was done was done. I don't think it sank in about Patsy and Evie, not really. He was caught up in his own world over at the university.

I got under the covers and snapped off my light.

He left his on. He sat on the bed in his shorts,

hands on his knees, leaning forward so he could talk softly.

"I'm changing my major," he said.

"Yeah?"

"I want to be a vet, Parr. I want to work on farm animals. I know a lot about livestock diseases already. I'm good at that sort of thing."

"What'll happen here?"

"There's Evie, and there's Cord. And Dad can hire help. He's going to have to anyway, or he's going to have to rent out some of the land."

"Didn't you hear what's going on with Evie?"

"That'll pass. I'm talking about the future. I'll be here to help out in season, and summers, for a few more years. That'll give Dad time to figure things out."

"Or have a heart attack."

"I can't help it. I don't want to be a farmer."

"Anna Banana change your mind?"

"Don't call her that. She helped me see things more clearly. She doesn't want to live on a farm, either. If you marry a woman who doesn't want the farm life, forget it."

"Marry her?"

"Someday. But even if I never marry Bella, I don't see myself living Dad's life. I want more for myself, Parr."

"Okay. I don't blame you."

"It doesn't mean you'll be stuck here. Don't *let* it mean that."

"I'll be the only one left."

"Evie will be here."

"I doubt it."

"You kidding? Evie loves this place."

"You used to, too."

"Not like Evie. . . . And Cord's a good farmer. Evie doesn't have to *date* him. She'll forgive all this."

"You think Dad will?"

"Dad is a practical man, Parr. He's not going to find a better worker than Cord."

"So you'll forgive Cord, too?"

"It's over where I'm concerned. You live here in this little world, you can't afford big grudges."

"Can you where *you're* going?"

"Don't sound so sour, Parr. I'll be around."

"Sure!"

"I *will*."

I said, "Put out the light, would you?"

"I know it's sudden, Parr, and I know how you feel, but Dad will work it out. We all have to live our own lives."

"When are you going to tell him?" I asked.

"Not this weekend, Parr. Mom and Dad are going through enough with Evie."

He snapped off the light.

I said, "Evie's going through a lot, too."

"Doesn't she know the Duffs by now? How'd she ever get herself mixed up in that?"

"I guess she couldn't help it," I said. "None of us seem to be able to help what we're doing."

"We're changing, that's why."

I was sound asleep when I felt the hand on my shoulder.

"Shhh, Parr, come into my room."

I got up and followed Evie down the hall.

"What time is it?"

"It's three in the morning. I'm sorry, Parr, but I have to tell you something."

"I didn't even hear you drive up."

"I walked up. The car's down in the road. I just came from Duffarm. Patty's mother's real ill. Her father says it's our fault she's had a breakdown. They're going to put her in some clinic in Kansas City. Patty's sick about it. The best thing I can do is just clear out!"

Behind her, on the bed, there was an open suitcase, packed. She was getting down her strongbox from the top of the bookcase, taking out money.

"Don't let Duff run you out of town!" I said.

"I was going anyway. After Patty gets out of

Appleman, he's sending her abroad to some aunt she's got in France. He says if she still wants to see me when she gets back, that's her business."

"Do you believe that?"

"No. But I want to go, Parr. How can I stay here now?"

"Does she want to go abroad?"

"It's not a case of what she wants, Parr. . . . My car will be over at the bus depot in King's Corners. I'm getting the five forty-five to St. Louis." She was looking in the bookshelf. "I need something to read while I wait."

"You going to leave a note for Mom and Dad?"

"No. Tell Mom not to worry. I'll be in touch. Tell Dad where the car is. You can drive it when you get your license, okay?"

"I *can*? Thanks, Evie!"

She was closing the suitcase.

"Go in and flush the toilet," she said, "in case Mom woke up."

She gave me a hug, put out her light, and pushed me toward the bathroom.

"Take care, Evie," I whispered.

"Thanks, Parr."

Yeah, thanks, I thought.

The whole damn thing was my fault.

28

It was still dark when the Kidders came for me. Even the roosters across the way were asleep.

Evie hadn't left a note, so I wrote one fast and left it on the table.

Evie's gone to St. Louis, so don't look for her. I'll explain later. She's okay. P.

I sat in back with Angel, our hands sneaking over to meet. I had on a suit and one of Doug's old ties. Angel was wearing a white dress, white tights, and white shoes, with a pink sweater, a pink cloth rose pinned to it. Her long black hair was just washed. I could smell the coconut shampoo she favored.

Mr. Kidder got right down to business. "We've heard the rumors about your sister, Parr, and we're sorry for your family."

"Thank you, sir."

"Now, I have heard the same thing said about Evie was said about the Duff girl on that sign. Was nothing on that sign said your sister had gone after Duff's daughter."

"That's what I heard, too," I said.

"So now this is just slander, and 'he that uttereth slander is a fool'!"

"Father reminded us of the Old Testament's words that 'whoso privily slandereth his neighbor,' him will the Lord cut off," said Mrs. Kidder.

"Yes, ma'am. Evie's gone, anyway. She took off."

"She *has*, Parr?" Angel glanced up at me.

I nodded.

"Can't say as I blame her," said Mr. Kidder.

"We just want you to know we were too hasty judging Evie," said Mrs. Kidder.

"*You* were too hasty, Mother. I never judged her. 'God is the judge; he putteth down one, and setteth up another.'"

"Poor Evie," said Angel. "If anybody'd said that about me, I'd like to die!"

"Well, she's gone to St. Louis instead," I said.

"She'll be better off away from here," said Mr. Kidder. "Buck Duff is not a fellow you want against you. . . . Did you finish planting with all this going on?"

"Nothing interferes with planting," I said.

"I was going to say if you had more to do, I'm finished over at the Fultons'. Bud went back to Columbia last night. But I could lend a hand, if your dad's not done."

"Thanks, he is. But I'll tell him that."

"We had fine weather, didn't we?"

"Yes," I said. Angel was squeezing my hand, sitting as close to me as she could get herself.

The sunrise service was in the tent lot in Floodtown where farmers brought in small crops at the end of summer, extra tomatoes, corn, cucumbers and other vegetables, flowers, and baked goods.

There was a post marking the highest point of the floodwater back in '73, which was the flood that wiped out the farms and homes of everyone in Floodtown. There was a wall behind that with a quote from Mark Twain painted on it.

One who knows the Mississippi will promptly aver . . . that 10,000 River Commissions . . . cannot tame that lawless stream . . . cannot say to it Go here or Go there and make it obey . . . cannot bar its path with an obstruction which it will tear down, dance over, and laugh at.

Under that were names of people who hadn't survived.

It was just getting light enough to see our way into the rows of folding chairs, facing a makeshift pulpit, with benches for the choir behind it.

The sun was rising in the sky at the end of Pastor Bob's short sermon about the meaning of Easter, and the choir rose and sang "I am Risen."

Then it was Angel's turn.

As soon as she got going, I knew she'd picked the hymn herself.

It was called "We'll Never Say Good-bye," and she looked right down at me when she sang the chorus:

We'll never say good-bye in heaven,
We'll never say good-bye (good-bye)
For in this land of joy and song,
We'll never say good-bye.

I went back to their trailer for sausage, eggs, and homemade biscuits, and then I asked Mr. Kidder if he'd mind driving me over to St. Luke's. I said that Easter Sunday meant a lot to my mother, that we tried to have the whole family together.

In the car he said, "I didn't want Angel to ride with us because I wanted to say something personal to you, Parr."

"What's that, sir?"

"Angel says you'll be getting your driver's license soon. I'm glad for you, because I remember myself at your age, champing at the bit to get behind a wheel."

"I'm going to have Evie's car," I said.

"I'm glad for you, Parr. But I got a rule and I don't want it broken. Angel's not to be out after dark in that car unless it's a very special occasion like a dance at her school or yours, and then you'll have to drive her straight home. No parking, ever, Parr. You know what I mean?"

"Yes, I do."

"I'm telling you this because the man's in charge of those things, and I hold you responsible, Parr. No parking, ever!"

"I heard you, sir."

"You hear me and you *listen*, Parr, or it'll be all over for the two of you."

"You don't have to worry, sir."

"I have to worry. Anyone's got a daughter has to worry!"

St. Luke's smelled like a funeral parlor with all the flowers everywhere, and every female wearing her best perfume.

All the women were dressed to the nines, but my father was wearing his old light-blue suit splitting at the arm seams, and Doug didn't even have a tie on.

Mr. Duff was in his center-aisle pew with Patsy. He had on a blue silk blazer with gold buttons, gray pants struggling to hold his big belly in, a red rose pinned to his lapel.

He was singing loud and shouting out all the responses, which was his way. He didn't glance our way as we filed into our pew. Neither did Patsy.

She had an early tan she must have gotten from playing tennis at Appleman, and her long blond hair was streaked with lighter shades through it. She was wearing a white shirt open at the neck, cut low, pearls, a yellow blazer, a navy skirt.

I kept staring at her and thinking of her choosing Evie to love, when she could have probably had any guy in the county she wanted, in the whole state of Missouri and maybe all of the U. S. of A.

I tried to fathom her state of mind from her face, but she didn't have any particular expression that gave a clue.

When the service was over, she didn't look in our direction once. She actually took her father's arm, and they made tracks, only stopping by the door long enough to greet the Reverend Southworth.

"I knew it would turn out this way," Mom said to me as we were heading down the aisle. "Evie's the one being run out of town, and *she* carries on like nothing's happened."

"Evie wanted to go. No one told her to."

"Oh, Parr, don't be so blind. What's Evie going to

do in St. Louis? Summer's coming—that was her favorite time on the farm."

"Maybe she'll come back."

"I could kill *you* for not waking us up!"

"Don't kill me," I said. "There's not a lot of us left to harvest."

Cord never showed up for the service.

I don't know what my father said to him, or what Evie did, either.

The next day when I got home from school, I saw he was back at work.

It wasn't that my father was a forgiving man. It was just that first he was a farmer. First and last, he was, and whatever was in between there wasn't time for.

The only mention of it Cord made was during an argument between us about who had to clean the farrowing floors, the worst job on the farm.

When my father wasn't within hearing range, Cord said, "You owe me, Parr. I took all the blame for the sign."

So I did them.

29

June, and Doug still hadn't told our folks about his decision to become a vet.

Evie called every weekend from New York City. She was staying at some women's residence run by the Salvation Army.

Dad was mad she was still gone, though in the beginning I think he was glad she was. I heard him tell her, "Well, you could use some salvation, I guess," handing the phone quick to Mom the first time we got a call from her.

He didn't want to get into a conversation with her. I don't think he knew what to say. His way of handling anything messy was to let it go by without discussion, what he called letting it work itself out, as though whatever "it" was had a life of its own.

He didn't think Evie'd stay away.

He thought she'd be back as soon as Patsy Duff left for Europe on July Fourth. After she graduated from Appleman, she and her father took Mrs. Duff to a rehabilitation center in Kansas City. They were due back in Duffton any day.

Evie had a job she said was temporary, working in a department store.

"What are you wearing to work?" Mom asked her.

I was sitting there waiting for my chance to say hello, and I muttered, "All you care about is what Evie's got on her back!"

"Your brother says I only care about what you've got on," Mom told Evie, "but that isn't true, honey. I'm worried sick about you. Be careful on the streets. People have guns, knives. You're too trusting, honey. You can't trust people in a city like that. . . . And something else, honey." I saw her look around to see if Dad had come up from the barn. There was no one else in the house but me.

Mom said, "Be careful of the friends you make, too, Evie. Don't seek out the gays. Think about that lifestyle, Evie. That's a very narrow life."

"Not like ours," I muttered. "Not like staying in Duffton, Missouri, on a farm, your whole life long."

Mom snapped, "Parr, stay out of this! Wait your turn to talk!"

Then she said to Evie, "Did you hear what I said? Don't make up your mind too soon that you're one of them. This could be a phase. You could be making a terrible mistake. Why don't you see a doctor, honey? There are clinics in a big city like New York, places you could go that charge fees according to what you can afford."

Whatever Evie answered, Mom shot back, "That's ridiculous! You haven't known anything of the kind all your life! . . . You just met the wrong person!"

Mom listened some more, interjected things like "Oh, sure, and where is she now? Did she stand by you, Evie? . . . Last time I laid eyes on her, she was hanging tight to her daddy's arm like she was his little girl!"

Finally, Mom gave up and passed the phone to me.

"We miss you," I said, because I hadn't heard anyone else say it. I meant it, too. Before, I'd only thought about Evie as someone to save me from being a farmer, but it was her presence I got to missing. I'd started thinking she was the only one in the Burrman family with any originality. My mother talked a lot about her being this stereotype, but it seemed to me that was what we were more than she was. At least she was in New York City. Not a one of us had even been there on a visit. Burrmans were farmers to our bones. We came from farmers, we bred farmers, we looked like farmers, and we'd probably die farmers— or I'd die trying not to be one: one or the other.

"Don't miss me, Parr. Think of me, but don't miss me. Get on with your life, and I'll get on with mine."

I wanted to tell her Doug and she were making it hard for me to get on with mine, but Doug had to break the news himself.

"Do you like that place, Evie?"

"I do, Parr. Sorry, little brother. I know you'd rather hear I can't stand it."

"Then you're staying."

"I'm staying. You get out, too, Parr, when it's time."

"You sound real happy, Evie."

"I'm not unhappy. . . . How's Dad doing?"

"He's doing. You know Dad. He does. . . . But he misses you. He can't ever say things like that."

"I know. But you'll all manage."

"We all manage, but we could sure use a repairman on the premises."

"You could use a repair*person*," Evie said, chuckling.

Mom hollered from her office, "That call is costing Evie money, Parr!"

No matter how often Mom told Evie to call collect, she never did.

I got my driver's license, took Evie's car to school, and found out right off the bat why Mr. Kidder had his rule.

I met Angel after. We weren't *parked*, not out by the quarry, anyway, where all the kids made out. We'd pulled over by a field halfway between Duffton and Floodtown, so we could watch some ponies gamboling in a pasture.

Angel was all over me, or I was all over her, or we were all over each other. We'd never really been off alone together, and we just let go.

I had to say, "Hey, wait!"

"For what?"

"Didn't you ever hear boys get excited?"

"Girls do too."

"It doesn't show, though."

"I like it showing." She laughed.

Having a car seemed to change her, but she said it wasn't the car. She said it was thinking about what was happening to her and me, Doug and Bella, and even Evie and Patsy. I'd finally told her the truth about my sister, making her promise not to tell her folks.

"Love is a force," she said. "It comes over you like waves crashing on a beach."

"Have you ever even seen a beach?"

"On TV. But you know, Parr, all the hymns I learn make me think of love more than God. Of what happens because of love. 'Love found me, My fainting soul was tempest tossed,' and 'Linger no longer, come come,' and 'I belong to him, yes, I belong to him.' I think about all that's happening around us because of love."

"You're not still afraid of Evie?"

"Uh-uh. I been thinking: What if it was a world

where males and females weren't allowed to love each other, and we felt like we do? I couldn't change. Could you?"

"No," I said.

"And I wouldn't want just any old boy, either."

"I wouldn't want just any girl."

"Not even Toni Atlee?"

"Oh, well, maybe Toni Atlee."

"Be serious, Parr."

"I wouldn't want anyone but you, Angel."

"So I bet Evie just wants Patsy."

"She did. I don't know about now."

"But I never would have had anything to fear from Evie."

"Right. Don't be too sure about me, though." I started the car. "You better stop learning those sexy hymns. They're going to ruin us."

She sang,

> *"I would not live without thee,*
> *not a day, not a day.*
> *I need thy strength to help me,*
> *all the way, all the way."*

I loved that voice of hers.

But I never could forget Mr. Kidder's voice, either. *The man's in charge. . . . I hold you responsible, Parr.*

30

Doug was home for the summer.

The last day in June, there was a benefit dance over at County to raise money for the coach there, who needed a kidney transplant. They'd opened the school especially for it.

I was getting dressed, picking Angel up at seven.

Doug had come up from the farrowing house as Dad was upstairs showering, and he waited until the water stopped running.

Then he called in at him, "We need a vet, Dad."

"*Now?*"

"Right now! How long since Doc Rothwell's been over here?"

"I don't remember."

"That's great. What's he running, some kind of fire-engine practice?"

Dad opened the bathroom door. "I call him when I need him."

"That's what I mean. You call him when the fire's already started. You seen those new barrows and gilts?"

"I was in the nursery not an hour ago."

"Well, they're in trouble. They been in trouble awhile."

"They're fine," said Dad.

"No way. They got something."

"You come back here hot from your college, you haven't been paying attention here, and you tell me—"

Doug didn't let him finish. "I tell you they're sick. *I'll* call Rothwell if you won't."

"You're not calling anybody!" I could hear the fear in Dad's voice, though. I could hear him stamping out into the hall. "What do *you* know?"

"I know a lot more than you do!"

"You don't know *anything*!" That was all we needed, sick pigs, and Dad couldn't stand hearing it.

Then Doug said, "It's your farm. I don't give a damn if you want to let them *all* die. Let them! I try to tell you something, and if you don't care to hear it, you give me a fight!"

"It's your farm too," Dad said.

"We'll talk about that. I'm calling Rothwell."

"Talk about what?" Dad said.

That was the start.

Rothwell got called, but while they were waiting for him to come from King's Corners, Doug blurted out that he'd changed his major . . . and his plans.

I didn't stick around to hear the rest of it.

That was the advantage of wheels.

You could just take off.

The first drops of rain started as I was heading toward Floodtown.

When I got there, Mr. Kidder was standing outside the trailer, under the tin overhang, looking up at the sky.

"You see that bank of black clouds, Parr?"

"It doesn't look good, sir."

"You be careful tonight. I think it's going to come down hard just about the time you're leaving that dance."

"Yes, sir."

"You're leaving at ten forty-five, Parr."

"The dance will go on until midnight, sir."

He ignored that. He said, "Unless it's really coming down. Then leave before quarter to. I'll expect Angel home at eleven thirty, earlier if the storm's heavy."

I was standing there under an umbrella, listening to the rain on the metal roof of the trailer.

Angel appeared in the doorway.

"Get her home safe and on time, Parr."

I said I would.

I meant it, too.

There was nothing then to make me think that wouldn't happen.

31

Kids who came to the County dances usually came in groups, boys together, girls together.

There were some couples like Angel and me, but Angel was the only one from King's Corners.

We didn't hang out with a crowd, so it was a while before the gossip drifted down to us.

It was Spots Starr who came up to us at the punch bowl.

By that time the thunder was crashing above us, and the rain was pouring down on the gym roof.

"Where's your sister tonight, Parr?" Spots asked me.

"She's in New York City every night now. Why?"

"My dad's been looking for Patsy Duff. They got back from Kansas City this afternoon and then she took off."

"Well, she hasn't been near our place."

"Oh, we know that," he said, as though he was working in the sheriff's office. "Mr. Duff thought Patsy was just going for a drive in the Porsche. Then he saw she'd taken all her luggage with her, still packed."

"I thought she was going to Europe," I said.

"So did he," Spots said. "She was supposed to leave for France Fourth of July. Then pffft!" He smiled with his perfect white teeth. He smelled of aftershave.

I shrugged, but my heart was racing. "She'll probably show up in time."

"My dad bets not."

"I don't know anything about it," I said.

"If we knew, we wouldn't tell," Angel put in.

"I know *you*," said Spots. "I saw you in St. Luke's last Christmas. You're from The Church of the Heavenly Spirit." He was looking all over her face.

"I don't know you," said Angel.

"He's the sheriff's son," I told her. And I told him, "This is Angel Kidder."

He said, "How come you wouldn't tell if you knew where they were?"

"We *know* where my sister is," I said. "She's not missing."

"How come you wouldn't tell, Angel?" said Spots.

"Because I'd let them alone."

"If they were together you wouldn't tell?" Spots asked Angel. He was leaning down so he could see into her eyes.

Angel shook her head.

"That isn't what they teach you in your church, I bet."

"I'm not *in* my church," said Angel.

Spots laughed. He said, "And I bet there's no dykes in your church."

"Why don't you go see?" said Angel.

"Hey!" said Spots. "You got your ruff up, haven't you?"

I could tell he liked Angel. He was giving her this lopsided smile, hugging himself, lightning flashing past the windows and he didn't even look out.

I got Angel back on the dance floor, and he tried to cut in a few times. We didn't let him.

We sat out all the Paul Joneses, too. We just wanted to be together.

We sat on a pair of folding chairs, trying to believe the thunder wouldn't come through the walls. It was already drowning out The County Seven, who were sounding the cymbals and drums every time there was another huge BOOM.

"I hope they're together," Angel said, and I didn't

have to ask who "they" were. "I'm on their side now, because I keep thinking what if it was us people were trying to stop."

I told her all about Cousin Joe in Quincy, the way Dad made fun of him. I told her I thought Dad was embarrassed by Evie now that she was out of the closet; it was *that* more than it was morals with him.

"It's morals with my folks, but I never told them Evie really is one—they'd die!"

"She's better off gone."

"I'd hate to be her. I mean, I'm *for* her, and I like her, but I couldn't stand being that way."

"When you first met Evie, did you think you'd hate to be like her?"

"I didn't think about it at all. I never would have wore stuff she wears, but I didn't think she was that different until the sign went up on the bayonet."

I took a deep breath. "I put it there," I said.

"You did not!"

"I'm telling you! I had some beers with Cord, and even though it was his bright idea, I went along with it."

"You did that to your own sister?"

"I wasn't thinking about what it'd mean to Evie. I didn't want to hurt Evie. I just wished I could get rid of Patsy Duff, so things would get back to normal on our place."

There was a great clatter of thunder and lightning underlining my confession.

I said, "I'm paying for it now."

"You mean the storm?"

"No. I mean the farm. I'm stuck with the farm."

The heavens must have liked hearing the truth. I got a few more claps of thunder for telling it.

At ten o'clock the principal at County took a bullhorn and announced the dance was ending because of the weather.

"Be very careful driving home, those of you who have cars. The buses are out front right now, waiting to load."

We lost the umbrella to the wind on the way to the Pontiac. We were soaked when we got inside.

"This is so exciting, Parr!" said Angel. "Turn on some music."

She was combing her wet hair and jumping up and down in the seat, and when I stuck the key in the ignition, she put her hand on my wrist.

"Not yet. Let's just stay here awhile."

"I got to get you home."

"We've got a perfect excuse."

"We can't stay long, though."

She was reaching for me, pulling me toward her. She whispered in my ear, "I've never kissed anyone with the sky lighting up like it is."

Around us cars were starting, and in the distance there was a roll of thunder.

"It's going away from us," I said.

"Don't you go away."

I don't know how long we were there before we heard the DJ interrupt a Billy Ray Cyrus song to say Illinois Route 57 down near Quincy was flooded, and power failures had plunged the area into darkness.

"We have to go," I said. "Now!"

"You're no fun, Parr."

"Didn't you hear what he just said?"

"Quincy's miles and miles away."

"Yeah, well, we're getting out of here!"

She sat very close, and we started off fine, but we were still outside Duffton when the rain washed across the windshield so hard I couldn't see.

Angel got very quiet suddenly, and I could feel her leaning forward beside me, as though she was steering the car, too.

"I *never* saw it like this," she said.

"I have to stop."

"Just pull over and stop."

"Where's over?"

I cut the motor.

"We're not going to make it unless this lets up," I said.

"Let's just wait, then."

It was eleven thirty.

We just sat there. We talked about the coming Fourth of July picnic out at the county fairgrounds. There was an amateur hour included every year, and I was trying to talk Angel into singing something. Both our families were going. Everyone was. Angel said it was too big a crowd, she'd be too nervous.

After a while we couldn't think of any more to say. The storm was getting worse. We couldn't see anything in the pitch black outside.

All I could think about was Mr. Kidder, and what state of mind he'd be in by then.

Whatever Angel was thinking about, it wasn't exciting her to touch me anymore.

"Daddy's going to kill me," she finally said.

"He's not going to kill *you*," I said.

We were still there at two A.M. when a highway patrol picked us up in a Land Rover.

Spots Starr was with the officer. "I knew you two were back this way," he said. "I saw you behind the gym when I left, so I knew you didn't get far."

They dropped me off before they took Angel on to Floodtown.

"Call me when you get in," I said helplessly. "I won't go to bed until I hear from you."

32

"That's for me," I said. The rain was still pounding down.

"We know who it's for," said Doug. "He's been calling here every hour on the hour."

"This isn't Mr. Kidder. It's Angel," I said.

It was him.

"This entire thing could have been avoided," he barked, "if you'd left when everyone else did!"

I began a lie. "We left right after every—"

He was wise to me. "I told you it'd be over between you two if you weren't responsible, so I'm giving you notice that it's over!"

I could see Mom in the kitchen, cleaning the mud off my good shoes. Our yard and driveway were mush.

"I'm sorry, sir. May I talk to Angel?"

Doug was sitting on the couch with his hands covering his eyes, as though he hurt for me.

"No, you cannot talk to Angel," said Mr. Kidder. "Not now, not ever again. I warned you, Parr!"

"I'm sorry, sir, but—"

There was a click, then a dial tone.

I put the receiver down.

Mom called in, "Now can we all go to bed?"

Dad was already there.

"He slept all through this?" I asked Doug as we undressed in our room.

"Dad sleeps off depressions. He took my news like a death in the family, went straight to bed after supper."

"Then he doesn't know Angel's father was calling here?"

"He doesn't even know about Duff's calls. Mom handled that. Duff's got an all points alert out on the Porsche. He doesn't believe Evie's in New York. He said there was no way Patsy'd drive all that distance. He thinks they're in St. Louis, or why would she have taken the car? . . . Mom had to give him Evie's number, finally."

"Do you think Patsy's on her way to Evie?"

"I give up on those two! I got sick pigs to worry about. Rothwell thinks it might be worse than I thought it was. Dad won't believe it!"

We listened to the radio in the dark for a while, heard a report that the Mississippi had risen over a foot already.

"I hope the levees hold," said Doug.

"What'll I do?" I said. "Go over there and try to reason with him?"

"Good God, Parr! Grow up! We've got more important things to worry about . . . like what are we going to do if this weather sticks with us for a while?"

"Why would it?"

"Why *wouldn't* it? And they've been watching that river since April. It was above the technical flood level at Quincy's lock and dam back then, and it hasn't budged. Now it's rising."

Mom poked her head in the door.

"You two stop talking. We've got a big day tomorrow."

I said, "Good night, Mom."

"Good night, honey. Don't worry, now. Mr. Kidder was just upset. Tomorrow he'll realize you two couldn't help that there was a storm."

"Yeah," I said. I didn't know how I was going to tell her about us staying behind the gym while the other cars left.

"Get some sleep, Mom," said Doug.

"I hope that phone's stopped ringing finally!"

We shut off the radio.

I whispered in the darkness, "What do you think Duff will do next?"

I couldn't get excited about the weather the way Doug did. I believed it was the farmer in him. Dad was the same way. They were always watching the sky, listening to weather reports, talking with other farmers about signs of hard winters to come—hornets building bigger nests, caterpillars furrier than usual . . .

They reminisced about old storms the way other people remembered their high school days or highlights of some years-ago World Series.

"What *can* Duff do?" Doug answered me. "He doesn't even know for sure Patsy's on her way to New York."

"My money says she is."

"Anyway, Patsy's eighteen now."

"I wish I was."

"Yeah, well you're sixteen going on twelve. You didn't come right home, did you? . . . We had another call I didn't tell anyone about. Spots Starr said you and Angel were still parked behind the gym when he left, and he left late."

"Living in a small town sucks!" I said.

"I hope you're packing condoms, little brother!"

"I am, but they're just for show."

"You better keep it that way."

"Something tells me I don't have a choice, anymore."

I said it, but I didn't believe it was over between Angel and me.

The rest of that early morning I dozed and woke up, dreaming I was with Angel, then blinking awake and trying to think of things to say or do to make Mr. Kidder change his mind.

When daylight came, more rain came with it.

33

Next morning after we finished our chores, Cord came up to the house with Dad and Doug and me.

The radio and local TV were calling for volunteers to help with the levee. There was talk of bringing in inmates from a boot camp out past King's Corners. The county jail had already sent over their prisoners.

"We should do some sandbagging ourselves," said Dad.

Cord said, "What we got to do is get the hogs to market."

"Hogs, pigs, the whole bunch of 'em," Dad agreed.

"The pigs have to be destroyed," said Doug.

"Not all of them!"

"All of them!" Doug said.

"Then we got to go fast," Cord said. "The roads are already clogged with farmers doing the same thing."

Without needing to be told, Mom was making coffee with Dad's contraband supply. "We're going to be all right here, aren't we? Douglas, I want some warning if we're not."

"I hope we are," Dad said. "The house is insured. The crops and livestock aren't!"

"The sheriff took Atlee's bulldozer to the levee first thing this morning," Cord said, "and *it* got stuck halfway there. This is *big*!"

"Thanks for telling us," said Dad.

While Dad and Cord were loading up the livestock to sell, Mom began making a meat loaf and some macaroni and cheese, in case we lost power later.

"What's going to happen to Melvin?" she said.

"Tomorrow we'll take him and the cows up to Yardley's."

I was changing into dry boots, planning on helping Doug with Atlee's livestock after Dad and Cord took off. They were being moved to higher ground over past Floodtown.

Later, I was thinking, we could go by Sunflower Park, see if there was anything we could do for the Kidders. I didn't think they'd refuse help, even if it was me. I'd heard over the radio some of the mobile homes were being hauled off, but most couldn't afford to pay the steep prices being charged: two and three thousand dollars—no way the Kidders could afford that.

Evie's Pontiac was still down on the side of the road.

I stood up and put on my poncho.

We heard a gunshot and Mom jumped.

"What was *that*?"

"Doug killing the pigs," I said.

She kept wincing while the shots kept sounding.

"That's all of them," she said, finally. She'd been counting. I hadn't.

"He had to," I said. "They were all sick."

Then an announcer's voice on the radio told us the fireworks displays and picnics planned throughout the area for the Fourth of July were all canceled.

34

Fourth of July morning.

"Parr, are you all all right?"

"We're all right. How about you, Evie?"

"Never mind me. Is the farm okay?"

"We're hanging in there," I said. "I just came in the door. Mom's down by the barn picking strawberries in the pouring rain, and Dad and Doug are sandbagging at the levee. A levee upstream gave way, so the river's rise has slowed some."

"*Picking strawberries?*"

"For freezing. What we can save."

I told her about selling the hogs and boarding

Melvin and the cows up at Yardley's, and that Mom had some of our valuables packed just in case.

I said, "Maybe the river will hold off. They got a hundred thousand bags on the levee. I was working up there last night. They had convicts up there with us: drug dealers, thieves right alongside farmers, forming a human chain—it's something else, Evie!"

I'd never gotten over to Sunflower Park. Anything personal was on hold. That had finally registered with me after I'd called Angel's number and heard Mr. Kidder bark at me to stop bothering people who had more on their minds than their own asses. I'd never heard him use the language he had, never imagined him calling me what he did: "selfish" being about the only word that wasn't obscene.

I hoped Evie wouldn't ask me about her car. The road where I'd left it was underwater now.

"What a time to be away!" she said.

"Well, you can always come home," I said.

"No, we can't," she said.

It was the first time she said "we."

I said, "How'd she get there so fast?"

"She flew from St. Louis on the first."

"Everyone was out looking for the Porsche."

"It's in a St. Louis parking garage now."

"Did you expect her?" I asked.

"It's been planned for a long time, Parr. The only

good thing about your weather is it's got Mr. Duff's mind off us. She just talked to him, so word will get out now where we are."

"In New York," I said.

"You're not going to believe this, Parr. I wanted to tell Mom myself. I'll call again tonight."

"Believe what?"

"We just flew out of Kennedy airport. We're on our way to France. I don't even believe I'm on this plane! Everything's happening so fast."

I said, "Evie? Good for you!"

"Do you mean it? I'm sorry about what you're going through there. I feel that I left you in the lurch."

"Don't worry about us, big sister. We'll handle it!"

"Parr? Thanks for saying that."

35

Where I saw Angel next was in a Salvation Army aid center in Dufftown, rummaging through a box of donated sweaters in search of one for her mother.

Sunflower Park was under ten feet of water. They'd lost everything and were staying in the V.F.W. hall at King's Corners.

We'd held out until the tenth, then moved over to the basement at St. Luke's church.

Angel's face didn't look glad to see me, so my own smile faded fast as I said, "Can we talk, Angel?"

"As soon as I find something here for Mama."

"I just picked up some sandwiches."

"When God gets you, He gets you good."

"It's the river, not God."

"Maybe it's God using the river." She found a pink cardigan and put it over her arm. We started walking toward the tent flap. She said, "Daddy says maybe this is to teach us something."

"I thought he believed sometimes things happen God just doesn't interfere with."

"For a reason, maybe," Angel said. "To warn us."

"Warn us what? That levees don't hold?"

"It doesn't have to do with levees. It's what people think they can get away with, and we get to thinking along with 'em they can."

It was raining outside. When wasn't it? We stood just inside the tent, out of the way of people coming and going. Angel had an old raincoat on, jeans and muddy sneakers. Her long black hair was held back by a red bandanna.

"Can we talk about us?" I asked her.

"I *was* talking about us. . . . Daddy's right, Parr. You should have been more responsible back that night of the dance."

"You wouldn't let me leave. Don't you remember?"

"I was just *with* you. I wasn't the one in charge, or driving the car. Maybe I didn't know better, but *you* should have. You're the boy."

I didn't know what to say to that. I was trying to think up something to answer when she put in, "Of course, who's the boy and who's the girl is all mixed up in some people's thinking. Some people think there's no difference, and I guess I got to thinking all kinds of crazy things myself, since I was actually cheering on your sister and Patsy Duff. I remember *that*. That was my own faulty thinking."

I put my hand on her shoulder. "Angel, you don't even sound like yourself. I know this has been awful, but don't start blaming it on things like Evie and Patsy and sin and bad thoughts. If you live in Florida, you get hit by a hurricane. If you live in California, it's an earthquake does you in. Here, it's the rivers. It's geography, not morality. Do you think *I'm* immoral?"

"That sign you put up wasn't moral, Parr, and it had to do with your own sister!"

"That's the thanks I get for putting my trust in you!" I said. "I never had to tell you I did that!"

"Daddy put his trust in *you*. A lot of good it did him!"

She'd stopped me cold.

I didn't want to argue with her. I was due back at St. Luke's with the sandwiches. Then Doug, Dad, and I were taking a joboat over to see if we could get into the house through the top-floor windows.

I said, "You're right about me not being responsible, and you're right about it being wrong to put up that sign. I just don't think it's right to blame this flood on God. All these people aren't sinners."

She said, "Not yet, maybe. But we were all heading in that direction. I'm not the only one saying it, Parr. A lot of people are asking, How come this happened?"

"This happened because we tried to turn the Mississippi into a canal, and it's a river!"

She was looking out toward the street, no expression on her face—until suddenly it brightened, but not because of what I was saying. She'd seen someone. She was waving her hand, smiling, finally, that old great smile of hers, like she was back to being her old self.

I saw Spots Starr heading toward the tent. He was grinning and waving, too. He looked the way I used to when I'd see Angel ahead of me.

"I should have known," I said.

Angel said, "You should have known to be more responsible."

"That, too," I said. "Definitely!"

That was the last time we talked.

It wasn't a time for talking, anyway, days that followed.

Things spoke for us.

Levees turned to Jell-O. Whole towns swallowed up. Dogs, cats, pigs, and deer clinging to rooftops. Corpses floating by, set loose from graveyards. People living in tents, attics, cellars, cars.

In the midst of it all, Will Atlee died.

"He was too late," said Dad. "He waited too long to go down to Florida."

"Do it now, whatever you've got to do," Mom said. "You'll never do it any younger."

"I've been doing it until this." From Dad.

Mom hooked her arm in his and said, "Me, too."

"Excuse me," I said, "I'm in the wrong movie. Where's the one about the rich advertising guy?"

"That must be a coming attraction," said Dad.

When we finally did get back inside our place, it looked like a shipwreck. We pumped water out for days, the odor of sewage and muck making us gag, everything we owned sodden, our walls covered with colonies of black, green, and purple mold and fungus.

"This is it!" Doug said. "This *does* it! Good-bye to this place forever!"

Nobody gave him an argument.

36

Evie came back for a visit in late fall.

"I wouldn't know this place," she said.

"You should have seen it a month ago," said Mom, "before Parr and Dad put on the new siding and Sheetrock."

"*And* Cord," I said.

Evie said, "Good old Cord."

"*He* hasn't deserted us," Dad said.

Doug was back at the university. Evie and Patsy were driving over to see him the next day, on their way to visit Mrs. Duff.

Evie brought Dad and me back black berets from Paris, and Dad was wearing his, eating lunch at the kitchen table. We hadn't laid new linoleum. The floor was scarred with marks left from mold and water damage. We'd nailed it back, what we could find of it, and we'd added planks from what was once our barn.

Evie'd let her hair grow down to her shirt collar. She had on tight black pants, Doc Martens, and a white canvas shell she'd bought in Rome.

She'd dropped Patsy off at Duffarm, one of the few places still intact after the floods. The Buick they'd rented in St. Louis was parked in what was left of our driveway.

Dad said, "How come you didn't bring us back a video of your travels? I think at least we deserve a travelog, being as we're never going to see Paris or Rome."

"Or Florence and Madrid," said Evie, "or even New Orleans, Miami, or Denver, Colorado, if you keep insisting on being farmers."

Evie couldn't believe we were rebuilding in exactly the same spot.

"What can travel around the world and still stay in one corner?" Dad asked her.

"You and your *National Geographics*?"

"A postage stamp," said Dad.

"That's about the size of it," said Evie. "How are you going to manage, Dad?"

It was the first time she called him anything. They'd been talking without him saying Evie or her saying Dad, even though I was Parr and Mom was Mom.

"Part of our deal was for Atlee to will us his prize breeders," said Dad, "and we got them to high ground okay. Eventually those hogs will buy a barn for more."

Sometimes I thought life was about trade-offs. A levee breaking would ease some lands, but drown others. A good neighbor's death would save our necks. A flood with all its hard lessons would soften our ways of looking at things.

Dad said, "Parr here has turned into a pretty good carpenter."

"We wouldn't have been able to start up again without Parr," said Mom.

"Parr's not going to be around forever," I promised.

"Nothing is," said Dad. "We learned that."

"Sometimes I miss this place so much!" said Evie.

"Good thing you came back," Dad said. "You won't miss it so much the way it is now."

"It's in my blood, Dad. I'll always come back, as long as I'm welcome."

"Evie"—Dad finally got her name out—"you're like the railroad worker's daughter who got tired of being tied down at home. You made tracks for a better station in life."

There we were, the four of us again, laughing around the table. It seemed like only the table had changed. We were using an up-ended hog crate in place of the one that had floated off.

Mom and I walked Evie down to the car, with Pete and Gracie chasing after us.

"You talking to Mr. Duff?" Mom asked her.

"If he talks to me, I am. We'll see."

"Thanks for the nightie, honey. I never had anything from Paris, France. . . . Did you buy yourself some new clothes?"

"I didn't buy myself a nightie." Evie laughed.

Mom said, "No, I didn't think that you did."

"Are you still seeing Angel, Parr?"

"She ditched me," I said. "I got ditched like your Pontiac did. . . . I'm real sorry about that."

"I've got no use for a car in New York, little brother. We'll be staying there now. We found an apartment."

Evie stood still and gave a last look around. Then she bent down to pet the Labs. "So long, you two."

When she stood up, she hugged me, then Mom. I think she was crying when she got behind the wheel of the Buick. I could feel tears starting to sting my eyes, too.

She sent us a little two-fingered salute and began backing out.

"Tell Patsy hi!" I shouted.

Mom started to walk away. Then she turned around, cupped her hands to her mouth, and called out, "Don't you two be strangers!"